CASEY CLUNES INVESTIGATES

A pregnant Casey Clunes investigates a case of baby snatching. Young Gemma Stebbings' baby has disappeared from the nursery at Brockhaven Hospital. But all the CCTV footage of medical staff and visitors reveals nothing — so where is baby Justin, and who is responsible? *In at the Deep End* finds Casey attending a reception for a Cambridge college's new swimming pool at Doughty Hall. Author Susannah Storey performs the opening ceremony . . . then her dead body is discovered, floating in the pool . . .

Books by Geraldine Ryan
in the Linford Mystery Library:

LEAVE OVER
CURTAIN CALL

GERALDINE RYAN

CASEY CLUNES INVESTIGATES

Complete and Unabridged

LINFORD
Leicester

First published in Great Britain in 2008

First Linford Edition
published 2012

British Library CIP Data

Ryan, Geraldine, *1951* –
 Casey Clunes investigates. - -
 (Linford mystery library)
 1. Clunes, Casey (Fictitious character)- -
 Fiction. 2. Detective and mystery stories.
 3. Large type books.
 I. Title II. Series
 823.9′2–dc23

 ISBN 978–1–4448–1186–5

Published by
F. A. Thorpe (Publishing)
Anstey, Leicestershire

Set by Words & Graphics Ltd.
Anstey, Leicestershire
Printed and bound in Great Britain by
T. J. International Ltd., Padstow, Cornwall

This book is printed on acid-free paper

Casey Clunes Investigates

1

A great deal depended on this undercover job. Even now, at the last minute, there was a real risk of blowing her cover. She only needed to remove her Victoria Beckham-sized shades or whip off the unflattering baseball cap beneath which she'd tucked her long hair and it would all be over. You never knew who was about at ten o'clock on a Monday morning who might be able to put a name to her face, even here in Steercroft, nine miles from home.

Thrusting a hand inside her bulging pocket, Casey's fingers closed tentatively around the fat white paper bag. Every nerve in her body tingled at the enormity of the spoils it contained. She itched to tear off the wrapping and inspect the goods right now. But then her sensible self kicked in.

'Wait till you get back to the station,' that sensible self urged. 'And for God's sake relax. All this stress just isn't good for you!'

Maybe she was going to have to learn to listen to Sensible Self more often. She could start by slowing down. It was a lovely day — hard to believe it was February. She'd take the scenic route through the park back to her car, she decided.

In the midst of the planning disaster that was Steercroft, the municipal park was an unexpected oasis of calm. Dropping down a gear from stride to stroll, Casey closed her eyes, all the better to appreciate the sun's warmth on her face.

Her mind drifted back to New Year's Eve. 'What will next year bring for us, Casey?' Dom, happy drunk on champagne. Everyone dancing, whirling round the floor. 'Haven't we got everything we want?' Herself, shouting over the din. And then he'd pulled her close and whispered, 'What about that baby we neither of us dare mention?'

Her reply had been flippant. 'What baby's this?' she'd said, like she'd never looked longingly at a beguiling infant

4

before and wondered if the time would ever come when she would hold her own child in her arms. A single moment passed. A heartbeat in which an unspoken contract was sealed. A feeling of elation that what she desired was equally desired by Dom; and in the hours that followed all caution blown to the wind.

Suddenly something struck her on the ankle, breaking into her reverie. They'd approached so stealthily, swishing over wet grass, and cutting a determined swathe through the pastoral idyll she'd managed to contrive for herself, that she only realised she was surrounded when she opened her eyes.

Her first instinct was to turn and run, but a quick appraisal of her attackers showed them to be equipped with nothing more threatening than a row of unarmed babies and toddlers in various prams and buggies.

'There she is!'

'Stop her before she gets away!'

'Don't think that disguise fools us!'

The posse of young mothers had her trapped inside a circle. The only way she could have escaped was by grabbing one of the buggies — the one that had rammed her on the ankle — and tossing it to one side. Not a move that would endear Brockhaven Constabulary to the public once the Press got hold of it, she quickly realised. Every eye was trained on her, each face stiffened with resolve. The only avenue left open was to wait for reason — theirs, not hers — to prevail.

'The police'll be here any minute so you'd better start getting your story straight,' said an older woman who, instead of being in charge of a buggy, had an unruly dog on a lead. 'Trying to snatch a baby just because you thought you could get away with it while his poor mother's back was turned! You and your sort should be locked up for life!'

'Whoa! Stop right there!'

Admittedly a little slow on the uptake, Casey had finally snapped into DI mode. Whipping out her ID card, she flashed it at the older woman, who she'd decided was the ringleader. 'DI Casey Clunes. Brockhaven Constabulary. Now will some-one tell me what this is all about?'

'Don't trust her,' someone else called out. 'Anybody can forge documents these days.'

A ripple of agreement passed through the crowd.

'Look,' Casey pleaded, 'have I heard correctly? Are you seriously suggesting I'm a baby snatcher?'

Her questions were answered by a wall of silent mistrust, finally broken by the dog owner.

'You'll be answering the questions not asking them when the police turn up,' she said. Adding, as the wail of the police siren grew louder, 'And you won't have long to wait either.'

★ ★ ★

If Casey had imagined she could slip back into the nick and take up where she'd left off, she hadn't reckoned on mobile phones and text messages. The first thing to greet her, pinned up on the notice board in the entrance to the station, was a pen-and-ink drawing of a woman — herself, obviously — in shades and baseball cap, the words *Have you seen this woman?* scrawled underneath.

Casey was angry with herself. The whole point of going nine miles out of her way to visit a pharmacy was so that she wouldn't be recognised.

Instead, she'd been held at buggy point, then had to explain herself to two rather stout WPCs who'd shot out of their car fully prepared to take down her particulars. Brockhaven was a small town. She knew all the assistants in Grundy's Pharmacy — if not by name then definitely by face — and they would have known her, too. Maybe not as Casey Clunes, private person, but very definitely as the DI from the Brockhaven force. Her face had been in the local newspaper three times in this last month alone.

What if one of the shop assistants was related to a police officer or to one of the many support staff employed by the constabulary? It could be all round the nick in no time that Casey had been in to pick up a pregnancy test.

Cautiously, she slipped her hand inside her pocket, to check the test was still there. Was it really such a good idea to do the test in the ladies' loos?

Now she was actually back at the station she felt herself chickening out. No. Much better to do it at home. More privacy for one thing. And no need to pretend that her life hadn't changed in a heartbeat either, and would never be the same again, if — and she was sure it would — it came out positive.

That decided, she headed for the canteen for a much-needed cup of tea, her strategy for dealing with any jokers already decided. What she did and what she wore to do it in on an early spring morning in Steercroft was nobody's business but her own. If anybody asked she'd tell them she was sworn to secrecy. She was a DI after all.

Never one to avoid confrontation, Casey took her cup of tea over to a table where a heated discussion was going on between a number of officers on their break.

'It's all very well putting up silly posters but just in case you've all forgotten, today isn't the first time a woman has been spotted trying to take a child away from its mother. It's a very serious matter.'

Casey recognised the speaker as WPC Gail Carter, just back from maternity leave, addressing her colleagues in that feisty way of hers that Casey remembered and cherished of old.

'Hey, Gail! Welcome back. We've missed you! How's the little 'un?'

For the life of her, Casey couldn't remember if Gail had had a boy or a girl.

'Sweet, thanks, Casey,' Gail said, falling to enlighten her.

PC Tony Lennon was stirring his tea, avoiding Casey's eye. 'What a giveaway, Tony,' Casey thought. 'You'll never make a criminal.'

'Not a bad likeness but don't give up the day job, Tony!' She flashed him a broad grin, which provoked jeers and hoots of laughter from the bystanders.

Tony protested his innocence good-naturedly, then gestured for Casey to sit down, whereupon she squeezed in between Gail and him.

'What do you know about these attempted baby snatchings, Gail?' Casey asked. 'It's been going on for a while, hasn't it?'

'Too long,' Gail reiterated. 'And we're doing nothing to stop it, strikes me, except put out statements telling mothers to be on their guard by all means but to remember that most of the sightings of this so-called baby snatcher appear to be unconfirmed.'

Gail drained her tea, set the cup down on the saucer with a clatter, and added: 'Patronising, paternalistic tosh, if you ask me!'

'Good to see maternity hasn't made you all soft and cuddly,' Casey said admiringly.

'On the contrary. I've got a baby of my own now, remember, and if anyone tried to take him away from me, well . . . '

'I expect every mother feels the same as you, Gail,' Casey said. 'And you're right. We've got to start being a bit more pro-active in trying to find this woman before she succeeds. As soon as we've had this tea, how about you and I go over all the witness statements?'

★ ★ ★

In the TV room of the maternity wing at Brockhaven County Hospital, a group of recently delivered mums were killing time between their late afternoon meal and visiting time. The topic of conversation was the shocking headline in the *Brockhaven Gazette* about the latest in a string of attempted baby snatches.

All the women, apart from one much younger-looking girl, were clutching their babies close, as if they were afraid someone were about to step from behind the curtain and make off with them.

'Shocking, isn't it!' said the woman holding the paper.

The women expressed various degrees of concern.

'Says here she's been spotted in Brockhaven down on the pier at least twice and in Steercroft Shopping Centre, too. And this is the second time in the park.'

'Well, I'm not taking my Carly out till they've caught her,' said one mother, stroking her baby's head.

Gemma Stebbings wasn't really listening. She just liked being here, in a group, accepted, no questions asked and no snide comments about her accent either.

'Manchester,' she'd said, when one of the others had asked her where she came from, and that was that. When they'd first got here, to Brockhaven, her and her mum, and she'd been forced to go to school because her mum said she wasn't doing no time for her if she was thinking about skiving off, you'd have thought she'd said 'Mars'.

'Small town people have small town minds,' Paul had said when she'd confided in him about the bullying she'd had to endure before she'd decided she wasn't going to bother going back to school any more. That was when she'd taken up wandering down to the harbour in the mornings, out of her mum's way. Where she'd met him. Paul. Her baby's father.

People with that mentality couldn't stand anybody being different from them, Paul had said on that first morning they'd met. He told her he should know because he was different, too. He'd been fishing. There was a plastic box on the ground next to him, full of brightly coloured wriggly worms tumbling about on top of each other. She'd been walking past, minding her own business, wondering how she was going to fill the empty hours between now and four o'clock when she could legitimately show her face at home again. When she'd looked down and seen them crawling about she'd shuddered and let out a scream of disgust.

Paul had laughed and told her not to be frightened. It was only bait, he said, and none of it could harm her. She stayed talking to him for ages. He was a good listener and when she said she wasn't going back to school ever, he didn't try to make her change her mind. 'You should always do what feels right,' he said. He told her he'd stopped going himself when he hit fourteen. He was seventeen now. A year older than she was.

'Gemma! Gemma! Are you with us?'

Someone was speaking to her. One of the nurses — the one with the big dark eyes who wore her glossy hair scraped back off her face, which should have made her look plain but didn't — was holding something out to her. A blue blanket. Something wriggling inside. She thought of the worms and how she'd shuddered that first time she'd seen them. But after that first time, she'd got used to them. Had even let Paul drop some in her hand, for a dare. This other wriggly thing, though — she didn't think she'd ever get used to that.

'Your baby needs feeding, Gemma,' the nurse said. 'Do you want to do it here or shall I take him back to your bed for you?'

Gemma didn't want either of these things. She didn't want to leave the other women. She felt safe here, listening to them chat. But everyone was looking at her so she had to say something. Grudgingly, she asked the nurse to take him back to the ward and she would follow.

'I wouldn't mind someone taking my baby away for a few hours if it meant I could have a bit of time to myself,' she said as she stood up to go.

It was obvious, from the shocked way

everyone was looking at her, that she'd said the wrong thing.

'It was a joke,' she said.

But she knew no one really believed her.

★ ★ ★

It hadn't taken Casey and Gail long to go through the witness statements, mainly because there was so little to go on. No pram or buggy had actually been wheeled away and no baby had ever — so far — been lifted.

'You can't really arrest a person for stopping to admire your baby,' Casey sighed.

'Plus we actually have to find her first,' Gail added.

'White, medium height, ditto weight, blonde hair, thirty-something. Wearing a navy blue jacket on one occasion and a beige coat on two others. Dark trousers or jeans, take your pick. Could be anyone.'

'Could be you,' Gail quipped, then, remembering Tony Lennon's poster, she blushed and began to apologise profusely.

Casey waved it away. Obviously she

wasn't going to leave the events of this morning behind her in a hurry.

'This woman — a Mrs Mandy Parker — says that she was on the pier with her baby in its pram. She thought she'd just pop into the Ladies to pick up some loo roll — never even shut the outside door behind her. She said Baby was dribbling all over her blanket.'

'Teething probably,' Gail interrupted.

'I bow to your greater wisdom,' Casey said.

Dribbling, teething babies. Wasn't she meant to feel all warm and maternal inside just at the thought of it? And if she didn't, did that make her a freak?

'Sorry,' Gail said, apologising for the second time. 'Touch of mushy mum syndrome.'

'It's all right,' Casey said. 'Anyway, when she came back out there was this woman, bending over the pram, messing about with the covers. Do you miss your baby when you're here, Gail?'

Her question had spilled out in an unprepared rush, taking herself by surprise as much as Gail.

'Like you'd never believe,' was Gail's reply. Her usually sharp features softened as she spoke. It was obvious she was lost in adoration. A complete goner.

'Must have been hard coming back.'

Gail nodded. 'Thankfully, he doesn't have to spend eight hours a day in a nursery,' she said. 'I've got family here. My mum has him when I'm here and when I have to work weekends Jim mucks in.'

'That's good, then.'

Casey forced a smile. Her own mother was dead and she doubted her relatives — none of whom she was particularly close to — would take very kindly to being asked to step in as full-time childminders once her maternity leave had ended.

Then there was Dom. She could hardly volunteer him as a candidate for a full-time house husband. Last year he'd moved to London, bored silly with writing reviews of amateur dramatics productions for the *Brockhaven Gazette* and craving the buzz that he was convinced only working for a national paper could offer him.

At the moment they weren't even living together — each commuting back and forth between London and Brockhaven whenever their busy lives allowed it, affirming before all their puzzled friends that their way of conducting a relationship was the spice that kept it sizzling and insisting it was everyone else's love lives that sucked.

Dom was coming down at the weekend. Her stomach gave a backward flip. By then she'd know the result of her test. How would he take it, she wondered, once theory became fact? Would the reassurance he'd given her on the last — and only — occasion they'd discussed parenthood, that whatever was cool with her was equally cool with him, still stand? Or would he be lying through his teeth when he took her in his arms and congratulated her?

'Are you OK, Casey?'

Gail's question dragged her back to the matter in hand.

'Fine. I was just trying to piece together all these sightings,' she lied.

'Except it's not possible,' Gail said. 'Different times, different places.'

'Whoever it is needs help,' Gail said. 'Quickly.'

★ ★ ★

Gemma lay on her bed, the curtains pulled around her so she could feed her baby in private. She hadn't wanted the nurse to go. Katerina, she called herself. From Romania, she said. Gemma didn't know where that was but she'd tried to look as if she did.

Katerina was brilliant with Justin. 'Why can't he be good for me?' she'd asked her as he twisted his small body furiously in a desperate bid to get away from her, or so it seemed to Gemma. Katerina had said feeding took practice, that was all, and all Gemma needed to do was relax, then Justin would, too.

She'd managed to feed him in the end, and done the winding bit. Katerina had congratulated her as if she'd done something really special. 'It's only a burp,' she'd snapped back, and immediately she knew Katerina was disappointed in her, just like the women in the TV room had been when she'd made that stupid remark about wishing someone would take Justin off her for a few hours.

He was quiet now. Or as quiet as he'd ever be, snuffling and rustling in his fish tank of a cot, more animal than human.

'You should always do what feels right.' Paul's words came back to her again.

She wouldn't have slept with him if it hadn't, in that little shelter he'd built out of reach of the wind and the rain and the smarting spray off the sea. It was her first time and afterwards he'd held her tight and told her he hoped it had been as special for her as it had for him.

They'd spent most of the summer together. Paul had lots of jobs to do but on most of them he'd taken her along. Her mother never asked her where she was going or who with. She'd never really been that kind of a mother.

She should be here now. From the sound of footsteps tripping eagerly into the ward and the raised volume of voices as people greeted each other, Gemma guessed it must be visiting time. Each time someone walked past her bed, she held her breath in anticipation, hoping her mum might pop her head round the curtain with a bunch of flowers or a great big box of chocolates. Ten minutes in and she gave up hoping. She must have had a better offer, she decided.

It was going to be hard bringing up this baby on her own. 'You'd better get used to it,' her mum had said, when she'd finally got round to telling her. Of course, by that time, she'd already guessed. 'I'm your mother,' she'd said. 'You can't keep secrets from me.'

The next day, she'd gone down to the harbour to find Paul and tell him, but he hadn't been there. Nor the next day. Nor any day after. She couldn't understand where he'd gone or why he'd left without a word, not after telling her how special she was to him. Her mother's laugh had been bitter when, sobbing, she'd said those words. 'That's men for you,' she'd said, giving her a knowing look. Like, finally they both had something in common.

She was tired, so tired. All she wanted was to go to sleep. She was glad when all the visitors left and the ward was quiet again. She heard someone push aside her curtain and mutter something to her, something about taking Justin to the nursery, and she snuggled down deeper into her bed. Without the baby disturbing her, she could have a proper sleep at last.

★ ★ ★

The first thing Casey did when she got home was check her answer machine. Nothing. Dom was probably propping up a bar somewhere, exchanging gossip with his newspaper chums. Enjoying the bachelor life while he was still able.

Casey grinned, kicked off her shoes and fell on to the settee. She was exhausted. But in a good way. Like she could go to sleep right now without even needing to carry out those rituals that had been part of her pre-bedtime ritual ever since she could remember. Things like removing her clothes and brushing her teeth, for example. Such a waste of time, all that business, she decided, as she drifted away into sleep. At the back of her mind, something niggled. There was something she should do. Some test or other. Whatever it was would have to wait until tomorrow, she decided.

She was having a dream. She and Dom were both on bikes. Dom was at the front and she was behind. Suddenly he called out.

'There's something ahead.' It won't get out of the way. Peering ahead, she saw it, too. A bundle in the middle of the road.

In her dream she knew exactly what it was. She knew she had to tell Dom to stop, but something held her back. Struck dumb, all she could do was listen to him ringing, ringing, ringing on his bell. The sound of the bicycle bell morphed into the sound of her mobile ringing.

It was the station.

She was needed at Brockhaven Hospital — and she was needed now!

2

'The hospital?' said Casey, trying to shake off the tide of sleep that was threatening to engulf her again. 'What's happened?'

'A baby has been taken from the nursery. A little boy.'

Casey's blood ran cold. 'I'll be right over,' she said, wide awake now. She was reaching for her coat even as she put the phone down.

★ ★ ★

Casey and the two WPCs who were accompanying her were shown into the small, sparsely furnished office that had been set aside for them at Brockhaven County Hospital.

The office was one of the few private places in the hospital, where Casey imagined anxious relatives paced for hours or sat, shuffling their feet, bracing themselves to receive bad news.

The mother of the abducted baby and a slightly older woman she initially assumed must be a friend were waiting for them, the bearers of no news at all so far.

Casey, in her warm winter coat, prickled with perspiration. Why on earth did hospitals have to be so overheated? On the wall, a framed landscape hung skew-whiff and a solitary dusty plant stood in the corner — someone's poor attempt at adding a homely touch to the place, she decided.

The anxious-looking, dark-suited official who'd welcomed them on their arrival, and whose job no doubt it was to ward off any accusations that the hospital had been at serious fault to let such a dreadful thing happen, hovered at Casey's shoulder. A ward sister held the young mother's hand.

The girl, shrouded in a voluminous pink dressing-gown, couldn't have been more than sixteen. Her skinny, pale, bare legs and fluffy pink-muled feet stuck out beneath its folds, lending her an air of vulnerability. When she lifted her eyes at Casey's entrance, they held such hope and desperation that Casey wished herself

26

a hundred miles away.

'No, Gemma,' she said. It was the last thing she wanted, to raise the girl's expectations falsely. 'I'm sorry. There's no news. Not yet.'

The girl's face fell and she cast her eyes back down to the floor, whereupon the ward sister gave her hand a comforting squeeze. The official cleared his throat as if he were about to speak, but seemed to change his mind when he caught the older woman scowling at him.

'Gemma Stebbings is the mother's name,' the duty sergeant had informed Casey, just before she'd made the dash to the hospital. 'Says that the last time she laid eyes on the baby was some time during visiting hour. Has a vague memory of someone wheeling him away from the side of the bed but didn't think of objecting because she assumed it was one of the nurses.'

'Is that still all you've got to say? My Gemma's beside herself waiting for news and I'm exhausted with the worry of it all.'

Now that the older woman had

revealed herself to be Gemma's mother, Casey searched for some trace of similarity between them.

Only the dark roots of her platinum blonde hair revealed her original colour to be an exact match for her daughter's. The rest of her — down to her heavily made-up face and orange fake tan — bore little resemblance to the girl with the pale complexion clutching the ward sister's hand.

'Mrs Stebbings, you can rest assured we're doing everything we can to find baby Justin,' she said, more for Gemma's benefit than for her mother's. 'There are officers combing this building and conducting interviews as we speak, and every inch of footage from every single CCTV camera the hospital possesses is being minutely scrutinised.'

'I'm going outside for a cigarette,' Mrs Stebbings said, sounding almost disappointed that, far from being lax, the police were working flat out to find her missing grandson.

Casey resisted the urge to tell her to take as long as she liked; it was a relief when she'd gone. She knew she shouldn't judge the woman, but it was hard to have sympathy with someone who seemed happy enough to hand over the comforting of her daughter to a professional. Not that Gemma seemed bothered by her mother's exit. She was far more concerned that the ward sister should stay with her than her mother.

'Don't get up,' she pleaded, as the ward sister let go her hand to offer Casey her chair.

The official was at Casey's side in a moment with another chair. She couldn't help feeling sympathy with the poor man, who clearly had to be seen doing something useful. The Press would have a field day once this story got out.

She accepted the seat with a gracious smile, before introducing herself to Gemma.

'My name's Casey,' she said in as reassuring a manner as she could muster, 'and I'm the Inspector in charge of finding your son.'

Gemma looked blankly at her. 'It's my fault he's gone,' she said, the words spilling out between sobs of anguish.

'They were talking. Earlier. About some woman who'd nearly snatched a baby in the park. And I said anybody could have my baby if it meant I could get a few hours' sleep.'

'You didn't mean it, Gemma. You were exhausted, that's all.' The ward sister threw Casey a pleading look as she spoke. 'Go easy on her,' it said. 'The poor girl's got no one on her side but me.'

'Sister's right,' Casey said. 'It was just a throwaway remark. Don't dwell on it. Try to think about how you can help us get your son back to you quickly instead. Now, I'm going to have to ask you some questions, Gemma.'

'But I've already said everything I know. How is me repeating things going to get Justin back?'

'It just might,' Casey said. 'Let's start by going back to the last time you saw him.'

* * *

'I'm on my way,' Dom had said. Just like that. No, 'Have you any idea what time it

30

is?' Nothing about his job having to come first just like hers always had to. Just a promise that he'd square it with his boss, get in his car and be in Brockhaven as soon as he could.

She'd worked all through the night. Everyone had. Off-duty police officers — including WPC Gail Carter, who was just back from maternity leave — had dropped any ideas they might have had of catching up on their sleep and begged to be allowed to join the hunt for baby Justin Stebbings.

Members of staff at the hospital had been questioned, lists of visitors' names had been drawn up, every detail significant or not had been noted. So far CCTV had thrown nothing up, but at this early stage of the investigation, there was a mood of optimism that sooner or later it would.

Gemma had been unable to add any more to her statement other than that she thought the nurse who had wheeled Justin back to the nursery might have been foreign. Since sixty per cent of the staff who worked on the maternity ward hailed from countries other than the UK, this extra piece of information wasn't as groundbreaking as Gemma had possibly hoped, but right now anything was better than nothing.

Back at her flat, as the daylight began to creep between the gap in her living-room curtains, an exhausted Casey had slumped on to the settee. She had to get some sleep. The hours ahead were going to demand everything she and her team had to offer.

The pregnancy test lay where she'd dropped it earlier. Reaching for it, she'd found herself once more reading the instructions.

Casey never would have said that she was a procrastinator. Quite the opposite, in fact. As a rule she liked to get things out of the way as soon as they came up so that she could move on to the next thing right away. But it was fear of the next thing that was holding her back from performing the simple operation of peeing on a stick. As long as she refrained, she didn't need to think of this baby as a reality. It was still within her power to deny the existence of that bunch of cells inside her. A bunch of cells that were multiplying even as she sat there doing nothing.

Meeting Gemma earlier had affected her deeply. Gemma's was a real baby — not a possibility like her own — and someone had stolen him away from her. Just hours before, that teenage girl had been wishing herself anywhere but in hospital and anything other than a mother, but with the baby's abduction something had changed. The invisible cord that bound her to her son had been savagely cut and she could never be whole again until he was returned to her.

Casey understood that now, had learned it from the anguish in the girl's eyes when she'd cruelly informed her that there was no news. Before she continued with this case, it was time to look her own future in the eye, she decided, as, prising herself from her seat, she made her way tentatively to the bathroom.

And it was on her return that she'd made that call to Dom. Because she was scared, and deliriously happy and full of awe and dread, and fending off so many other conflicting emotions all at once that she couldn't put a name to, and she needed Dom, who was good with words, to help her work out exactly how she felt.

★ ★ ★

La Copa served the best cocktails in Brockhaven, Dom insisted, so this was where the two of them now sat, in an alcove looking out on to the darkening high street. Not that Casey could drink, of course, she reminded Dom. One — she had a second long night ahead of her after a busy afternoon, and she needed to keep her wits about her. And two . . .

'Well, you know about two,' she said, reaching for his hand across the table.

'A small one wouldn't hurt, surely,' Dom said.

Dom was a man who thought it was OK to offer sausages to their veggie friends at barbecues because there wasn't much meat in them.

Casey made a face that suggested she thought he was a lost cause. If she was naïve about the dos and don'ts of pregnancy, she had a shrewd idea that Dom was going to find the journey even more bewildering.

'We'll put you in charge of refreshments at the AA Christmas party, shall we?' she said.

Dom grinned. When someone — Casey thought she recognised him as the manager of the bar — arrived to take their order, he passed on the cocktail and ordered an Americano, same as Casey.

She was touched by his gesture of solidarity. She hadn't known exactly how he would react when she broke the news to him this morning. It was a coward's way out, maybe, to tell him as the two of them crept beneath the bedclothes and turned to each other as a precursor to making love.

The bedroom curtains had been closed and the room was still dark, so she hadn't been able to see his face as he registered the news. But he hadn't pulled away from her. Instead, he'd done that corny thing that the guys do in the movies where the father-to-be lays the flat of his hand on the woman's tummy and, between pats and chuckles, proudly calls her Mummy.

She knew then that everything was going to be all right. He was meant to be going back to London after this coffee had been drunk, and she was expected back at the station. Maybe it was the nature of the case she was dealing with, but for the first time since she'd been promoted, she'd have given anything to stay here with Dom, just making plans.

'That guy,' Dom said playfully as the waiter moved away. 'He smiled at you. You smiled back. Is there something you're not telling me?'

The trouble with living and working in such a small town was that it was almost impossible ever to separate business and pleasure. She'd met Graham Marchbank before, she told Dom. He was manager of this place. A couple of months ago he'd been punched in the face for the privilege and ordered to empty the safe.

'The thief got away with thousands. It was around Christmas so the safe was bursting.'

'Did you get the guy who did it?'

'Not yet,' she said. 'But we will.'

She'd interviewed Marchbank herself, shortly after the incident. He'd been badly shaken up, with a cut so deep above his eye it had almost closed it. A slightly built man, he wouldn't have put up much resistance to the thief, she'd guessed, although he insisted he'd twice refused to open the safe. It was at the third refusal that the interloper — who Marchbank had decided must have been hiding out in the men's toilets, waiting for the rest of the bar staff to leave before putting in an appearance — had hit him.

'Anyway,' she said, 'enough of that. It's only money and there's always the insurance.'

'You're still thinking about the stolen baby.'

Marchbank was returning with the coffee. As he set down Casey's cup he spilled some into the saucer. Apologising profusely, he offered to replace it, but Casey, doing her best to contain her irritation, insisted everything was just fine. She wanted to spend what little time was left with Dom, not getting into a conversation with Graham Marchbank about the robbery.

'Bag of nerves,' Dom said. 'Did you see the way that his hands shook?'

'That's what being a crime victim can do to you,' Casey said, mopping up the spillage with a paper serviette. 'It destroys your peace of mind and eats away at your self-confidence.'

She took a sip of her coffee. It tasted awful. Metallic. And the smell was quite disgusting.

'Delicious coffee,' Dom said, then, as Casey's expression registered, he added, 'What's up?'

'I think I've suddenly gone right off coffee,' she sighed.

★   ★   ★

To Graham Marchbank, it was a relief when the couple rose from their table and left. He'd nearly died when he'd recognised the tall, not bad-looking woman as that CID officer who'd come to interview him about the robbery. She'd sat and listened, gently prompting him to fill in the gaps, as he told the tale he'd rehearsed with Valentin till it was word-perfect, just before he'd made the call to the police. She must have believed him, since he'd had no other visits since then and it had been — what? — six or seven weeks now.

This evening she'd looked like she had more important things on her mind, which probably accounted for her apparently not even recognising him. The last time they'd met he'd had that eye to show her. He had Valentin to thank for that, too. 'What you complain for?' Grinning down at him, while he'd picked himself up off the floor, reeling from the pain. 'Trust me, my friend, I know what I'm doing.'

Psycho, that Valentin. But just what you wanted for a bouncer when things looked like they were about to kick off. There was never any trouble when Valentin was on the door. Built like a brick wall, for one thing. Then there was that mad gleam in his eye that had a tendency to sober people up.

To be fair to Valentin, it looked like the punch in the face had done the trick the night of the robbery. The copper had even handed him a card when she'd got up to go. Victim support. They'd had a laugh about that. It was at such moments that he'd felt close to Valentin, grateful for everything he'd offered to do for him and Vanessa.

Not that Vanessa knew anything about the robbery. He'd never tell her how he and Valentin had plotted it for days beforehand. But it had been for her he'd done it, to make her happy and to get her what she wanted more than anything else in the world.

When you were the manager of a bar like La Copa that opened from eleven in the morning till gone two at night, it was difficult to find time for friends. The bartenders and the waiters were good lads. But they were younger than he was and their concerns were different. Valentin had become his confidant. Big and solid, with not much of a command of the English language, he'd been a pair of ears at the end of the day after everyone else had gone home.

He'd taken to offering Valentin a drink,

ostensibly as a thank you for keeping the place trouble-free. But the truth was he was desperate for company and — if he was honest — for a reason not to go back home to Vanessa, and all the hard work that entailed.

He must have had a few that night or he'd never have opened up so freely about all the bad stuff that was going on in his life. The credit-card debts he was no more capable of paying off than he was capable of that other thing. Giving his wife the child that she'd been longing for for the best part of their seven-year marriage.

Valentin had listened as Graham had explained exactly how much money he'd laid out over the years so that Vanessa could have the fertility treatment she was convinced would work, even for that third time, after it had spectacularly failed on two previous occasions.

He wasn't a rich man, he'd explained to Valentin. He'd borrowed money on every card he could. He wouldn't have cared about the debts if the treatment had worked — he would have paid it all back somehow.

But it hadn't worked and it wasn't going to work. On their last visit to the clinic the doctor had advised them to think about adopting, but Vanessa wouldn't countenance it.

'It's a baby she wants,' he'd told Valentin, 'and in this country, tiny babies to adopt are in short supply.'

'Not in Romania,' Valentin had said. 'In my country there are many unwanted babies. Just say the word, my friend, and I can help you get the baby of your dreams.'

Of course, he'd laughed it off that time. But then there'd been the incident on the pier, when she'd almost made off with that baby. There'd been other times, too. That's when he'd gone back to Valentin, and between them they'd come up with the idea for the fake robbery to finance the adoption that Valentin had offered to take care of for them.

He'd thought they were out of the woods, once the deal was sealed. But even yesterday, when Vanessa had known that very soon she'd have her own baby in her arms, she'd played that stupid trick again, although she strongly denied that she'd intended snatching the baby from Steer-croft Park, whatever witnesses to the event had said.

'I was only looking, this time,' she'd said. 'I just wanted to imagine what it would be like to take my own baby out for a walk in his pram.'

He loved Vanessa. But sometimes he wondered how much more he could take.

★ ★ ★

Katerina Iliescu forced herself to get out of bed and shower. She had to go back to the hospital to do her shift, to act as normally as possible. Those had been her orders from Valentin. He'd know if she didn't go in. Hadn't he already said he'd come looking for her, to check that she wasn't thinking of doing something stupid like running away and thus drawing attention to herself?

But she still couldn't eat. The last thing she'd tried — the white, English bread that tasted of nothing but air — had sent her rushing to the bathroom, where she'd been violently sick.

The shower soothed her jangling nerves. She even managed to forget, for moments at a time, the dreadful thing that she had done. But then, as she changed into her uniform, she was reminded of the night ahead, and she began to tremble as she did her buttons up. How on earth was she going to get through this shift when all the talk would be about that missing baby?

Would she still be there at the hospital, the mother? How could she look her in the eye after what she'd done? How could she look anyone in the eye — the midwives, the other nursery nurses who'd always been so kind to her?

What a fool she'd been to believe Valentin when he said he'd help her. A man like that would only ever help himself. Throwing herself down on to her bed, Katerina sobbed for herself, and for the poor young mother whose baby she had stolen. The baby himself was safe and well — she'd been assured of that. But what about the girl, little more than a child herself, who'd given birth to him? What would become of her?

3

Casey prayed that Gemma would be able to dredge up enough strength from somewhere to keep it together for the cameras, who were shortly due to arrive, just in time to roll out her appeal on the lunchtime news. So far this morning she'd said not a word but simply stared ahead, tears rolling down her face from a seemingly inexhaustible supply.

WPC Gail Carter — who'd managed to persuade Gemma out of her dressing gown and into her ordinary clothes — said, 'It might be that she won't be able to go ahead with it. Maybe we should get her mother ready as a standby.'

Casey shook her head vehemently.

'No way,' she said. 'We want people to realise the urgency of finding this baby and only Gemma, as the mother, can get that across. Dawn Stebbings would love the limelight, I'm sure. But she'd just see it as a photo opportunity. I don't think she cares enough, frankly. Not for Gemma and not for Justin either.'

'You're probably right,' Gail said. 'But if Gemma breaks down in the middle of it . . . '

'Then one of us must be on hand to supply the important details.'

Gail said that, as the senior officer, Casey ought to do it, but Casey said that Gail, as a mother herself, might be better equipped to prompt Gemma if she started to unravel. In the end, they tossed for it and Casey, who hated cameras, managed to get out of it.

'D'you think anything will come of it?' Gail asked her later, as they looked on while the cameraman attached a microphone the size of a charity pin to Gemma's shirt.

Casey shrugged. More than thirty-six hours had passed since this baby had been stolen. Justin was tiny and vulnerable. If he became ill, would the person who'd taken him have the common sense to seek treatment for him? Would they even have the nerve, knowing that every GP and baby clinic in the country was now on red alert in case the baby was presented at their surgery?

'We just have to hope, Gail. That's all we can do, for poor Gemma's sake.'

★ ★ ★

Vanessa Marchbank was ironing her husband's shirt. Graham was making them both a quick lunch before he went into work. Unfortunately, there was no one who could relieve him as manager at La Copa at such short notice, he'd explained, but he promised to get something organised so he could take some time off very soon.

A tangle of newly washed baby clothes and underwear overflowed from the wicker laundry basket at her feet and spilled over on to the carpet. The steam iron gave off the slightly scorched smell she loved, which mingled with the appetising aroma of bacon wafting from the kitchen as it sizzled in the pan. A new emotion stirred within her. She was content at last.

She should have felt exhausted. 'Have a

lie down while you have the chance,'
Graham had said to her, after she'd
changed little Georgie — the name they'd
both agreed on for their baby — and put
him down for a nap. He'd volunteered to
bring her sandwich up to bed for her but
she'd refused. She liked feeling tired and
busy and weighed down with domestic
chores. This was the real stuff of mother's
lives and she was a real mother herself,
now. Finally normal.

She reached for the remote control and
magicked the TV on. She'd been so
caught up in her own world these past
few days that she hadn't a clue what was
going on elsewhere. First there'd been
that unfortunate incident in the park.
She'd managed to give those women the
slip in the end but it had been close. All
she'd wanted was a peek; she'd meant no
harm. As if she'd harm a baby, knowing
how hard they were to get — for women
like herself, anyway. Barren women. She
shuddered at the cruel, old-fashioned
word as she trawled through the stations
for something uncomplicated to watch.

Here was an old episode of *ER*. How

young the cast looked then! She'd have liked to watch it but it was already well into a complicated story and at the moment she had the concentration span of a flea. Besides, she needed to keep her ears sharp for Georgie in case he woke from his nap and didn't know where he was.

Flick, flick, flick. A soap, another soap, tots' TV — she'd already made up her mind to severely limit that for Georgie. Local news. That would do. Not that anything ever happened much round these parts other than road accidents, a bit of flooding and the odd visit from minor members of the Royal Family.

A girl with long, lank hair that almost hid her face was leaning forward. There were people on either side of her. Everyone looked serious, like someone had died. The girl had tears streaming down her face. She was waving her arms in the air. Vanessa raised the volume.

'Please, please, please! I'm begging you. If you've taken my baby, I understand why you've done it and nobody — not me, not the police, not nobody — is going to punish you for it. All I want is my Justin back, safe in my arms.'

Vanessa listened, fascinated. The girl didn't look old enough to have a baby. Her voice was high-pitched, whiny and she mangled her words the way kids did these days. Even so, you had to feel sorry for her.

'Justin needs to be with his mother,' she went on. 'If you know anything about babies, you'll know just how important it is for a baby and a mother to bond.'

She'd been coached, obviously. There's no way she'd thought up that psychology stuff on her own. There was a pretty woman police officer to her left, and a man in a suit to her right. No doubt between them they'd given her the words. That'd be why they were there — to prompt her in case she forgot. She obviously wasn't very bright with her 'not nobody'. There didn't seem to be a husband on the scene either. Girls like that — easiest thing in the world for them, having a baby, while she . . .

Now she was describing him. A shock

of jet-black hair. Just like Georgie, Vanessa thought fondly. Neither she nor Graham had hair as dark as his and at first she'd been disappointed that the baby hadn't shared any of their particular features. But, as Graham had explained, when the opportunity of getting a baby from Romania had come up so suddenly, he'd had to tell Valentin to go for it. It might be weeks, months even before another chance came up, he'd reminded her, and they were in no position to be choosy about whether a baby's hair was the exact shade of brown to match Vanessa's.

What was that she was saying now? Vanessa stiffened and her flesh began to crawl as the young girl's next words began to sink in.

'He has a birthmark. It's quite distinctive but you wouldn't see it until you changed his nappy or put him in the bath.'

Graham was at the living room door, holding a plate in each hand, each stacked with bacon sandwiches. His attention was caught by the girl on the

TV screen who was bellowing her words now, thanks to Vanessa, who'd turned the volume up to full.

'You'll wake Georgie,' he said.

She cut across him with her next words.

'Shut up! Shut up and damn well listen!'

Graham stayed where he was, balancing the two plates in his hands. As his eyes flickered between the screen and Vanessa, he tried to make some sense of why, exactly, this girl's words were having such a dramatic effect on his wife. He caught the words 'strawberry mark' and 'as big a tenpence piece' and 'on his bottom'. There was a telephone number to call and then the picture changed to a serious-faced announcer back at the studio. Vanessa had gone white. She looked like she was about to faint. Why on earth was she staring at him so accusingly?

'You've never changed his nappy, have you, Graham?'

What had he done wrong now? he wondered. Hadn't he just made her this sandwich? Which, by the way, was getting cold. Was all this because he couldn't get the time off to give her more of a hand?

Holding out the plate to her in an appeasing gesture, he told her to forget the ironing and sit down. She came at him before he could stop her, sending both plates flying. A rasher of bacon had draped itself over the settee; one of the plates was in bits; he couldn't see the other one. And scattered all over the floor — like wounded soldiers on a battlefield — lay slices of bread, dripping in ketchup.

★　★　★

The area that had been set aside at the hospital as an incident room hummed with activity, most of it, as far as Casey could work out, pointless. CCTV had come up with nothing at all. Just reams and reams of poor-quality images of medical staff and mothers and visitors all going about their business, that's all.

If, so far, there was no answer to the question who, at least there was no reason to ask the question why. People stole babies because they were desperate to be given the opportunity to pour out all their love into one tiny, helpless little soul. It was this certainty that was so far keeping Casey optimistic and it was something she kept reminding Gemma of, in a bid to raise her spirits too.

It was only a matter of time before this woman's conscience kicked in, she'd reminded her. She must have seen Gemma's appeal by now. Then it would start to hit her that in fulfilling her own needs she was denying the real mother hers. When she'd voiced this theory, Gemma had fixed her with a desperate look and told her that she hoped she was right.

Her head was beginning to ache and she badly needed to stretch her legs. There was a water cooler at reception, if she remembered correctly. Stifling a yawn, Casey got up from her computer screen.

She heard the man's raised voice before she saw him. He was leaning up against the reception desk — a giant of a man — one huge fist rhythmically striking the desktop as he made his point in strongly accented English.

The receptionist shrank behind her

computer screen, a look of barely controlled terror on her face. Rows of patients waiting for their appointments glanced up occasionally from behind the pages of their magazines, or stared straight ahead, pretending not to notice anything out of the ordinary. Clearly, no one wanted to get involved.

Casey, however, had no such compunction, but she knew better than to march up to such a well-built, irate man with all guns blazing. If something was upsetting him, he needed to be calmed down with a sympathetic smile and a listening ear. Strolling towards him, she introduced herself and asked if there was anything she could help him with.

'I come here to look for someone is all,' he said, making some attempt to collect himself once he'd understood the identity of the woman standing before him. 'And this girl here — she refuse to tell me.'

'I've said many times that I'm not at liberty to divulge the whereabouts of members of staff to complete strangers,' the receptionist said, with a resurgence of confidence now that Casey was on the scene. 'It's against the law.'

'She's right, you know,' Casey said, trying out her most disarming smile for effect. 'Data Protection Act 1998. Perhaps you should give it up as a bad job.'

The man must have realised that he was beaten. Taking a step back from the desk and lowering his gaze, he mumbled something about not wanting any trouble, before clicking his heels at the receptionist and going to the exit.

'Weirdo!' the receptionist said decidedly. 'He's been on the phone asking for one of our nurses twice already in the last hour and I gave him short shrift, I can tell you. Never occurred to me he'd come round here looking for her.'

'Well, he's gone now,' Casey reassured her. 'I doubt he'll be back.'

In the course of her job, Casey met hundreds of people. This guy — didn't she know him from somewhere? Somewhere she'd been just recently?

'Who did he want, anyway?'

'Katerina Iliescu. Told him she wasn't due in till later and if she wasn't answering her phone at home it probably meant she didn't want to speak to him.'

'Ouch!'

The receptionist grinned. 'Yeah,' she said. 'Maybe that was a bit harsh. But he was really winding me up, you know?'

'So were you telling the truth about her whereabouts?'

The receptionist shook her head. 'Far as I know she's in. She works in the nursery. But like I said. Data Protection. And he's probably stalking her.'

Casey wasn't going to get involved in any fantasy the receptionist might choose to concoct. She still hadn't had her water and her head hurt even more. It was only later, back at her desk, as she sat monitoring all the calls that had begun to flood in as a result of Gemma's appeal, that she remembered where she'd seen that guy before.

It had been at La Copa, one very late night. Someone's hen night? Oh, God, yes. Beverley, one of the Community Support Officers. What a night that had been! Some drunk had tried to hit on one of the girls in their party. It was all under control, though, and the guy was harmless enough.

This other guy — the bouncer, so it turned out — descended on them out of nowhere, terrifying the poor drunk by wrestling him to the ground. There'd been no need for such force, and maybe Casey should have done or said something at the time. But it was Beverley's party and she hadn't wanted to spoil things for her. If this girl Katerina had upset this guy for some reason, then the receptionist had done a fine job in keeping him away from her.

★ ★ ★

Vanessa had locked herself in her room and insisted she wasn't coming out until he took that baby back. So much for motherly love. He'd confessed then. Surely, after everything he'd done to support her all these years, she wouldn't turn her back on him now he'd explained about the bogus robbery and his fears that Valentin would use it to blackmail him?

They were a team, right? For better or

for worse, wasn't that what marriage was all about? But all he'd got from her was an order to leave her out of it. None of this mess was anything to do with her. So much for loyalty, too.

Valentin had taken him for a fool. Ten thousand pounds he'd got from him. Plus knowledge that he'd single-handedly faked the robbery that had supplied the money in the first place — knowledge he could use against him. There was no proof at all that Valentin was involved with snatching this kid. It was him, Graham, who'd been left holding the baby, after all.

At first, on the phone, Valentin had denied everything, insisting he'd kept his part of the bargain. Graham had seen the courier twice, with his own eyes, hadn't he? — talked through the arrangements with her and everything. Was he calling him a liar?

If Graham had been face to face with Valentin he wouldn't have had the courage to fly at him the way he'd done then. But right now his fury knew no bounds.

'I don't know who she was but she was no courier,' Graham had snapped, his whole body shaking with anger. 'You can't fool me any more, Valentin. That baby has a strawberry mark exactly the same shape and in the same spot as the baby that's gone missing from Brockhaven General. Now, how do you explain that?'

Valentin didn't explain it at all. On the contrary, he hung up, leaving Graham staring at the phone and wondering what on earth he was supposed to do next.

That girl — Katerina. He'd had her down as a good soul. Young, quiet, very pretty. That first time he'd met her with Valentin. She'd come to the bar. Wouldn't have a drink. Only ever spoke when she was spoken to and all the while casting sidelong glances at Valentin as if to check with him that she was doing all right.

The second time he'd gone to her flat — to pick up the baby — Valentin was in an expansive mood, offering him a cigar to celebrate. The new daddy. Katerina had just flown in with him, he said. She'd hovered in the background, holding the baby confidently, patting his back to calm him down, singing him a lullaby as she walked him round the flat.

How could such a gentle girl as that — who'd talked him through the baby's routine and told him that there was absolutely nothing to be afraid of when he hesitated to take him from her, because babies were tougher than they looked — how could she have got herself involved with someone like Valentin? Did he have a hold over her too, just like he had over him?

All these thoughts milled round his head as the afternoon drew on. When Georgie/Justin woke, he fed him. Then he changed him. Then he lay him across his lap and poured out his heart to him. 'What am I going to do, Georgie?' he asked him. Georgie blew a raspberry from both ends by way of reply.

It was almost dark when he drew up outside Katerina's flat. Vanessa was still refusing to come out of their bedroom and, anyway, she'd made it clear she'd no intentions of offering him any help.

The more he thought about Katerina

and her wariness whenever Valentin had been around and how quickly she relaxed on the two occasions he'd left them alone with the baby, the more he was convinced she'd been coerced into taking part in the baby-snatching. Maybe he could talk to her and together they could come up with a plan to return the baby safely without implicating themselves. Maybe together they could even think of a way of getting their own back on Valentin.

The door to Katerina's downstairs flat was ajar, which was odd. Cautiously he pushed his way in, calling out Katerina's name. He thought he heard a reply of some sorts — a moaning, gurgling sound. Something crunched beneath his feet as he stepped over the threshold, and he placed a protective arm around Georgie, whom he'd transferred from the car seat to the baby sling, while, with the other hand, he groped for the light.

There, on the floor, in the middle of the living room which had been turned over so thoroughly that it was unrecognisable from the neat-as-a-pin habitation he'd seen before, lay Katerina, her body skewed at an awkward angle and her beautiful face covered in congealed blood. His heart thudding so loud he thought it would explode, Graham dashed forward and fell at her feet.

4

I just hope all this publicity doesn't bring Wayne down here looking for me.'

Dawn Stebbings scrabbled impatiently for her cigarettes on the settee. It hadn't escaped WPC Gail Carter's notice that since the three of them had arrived back from the hospital three hours previously, Gemma's mother hadn't budged once from this spot.

Clearly the woman imagined that part of Gail's brief as liaison officer was the endless rustling up of cups of tea and sandwiches for her.

Gail asked Dawn who Wayne was.

'My ex,' she said, her eyes alighting on the cigarette packet. 'The man we came down here to get away from.'

Gemma, heavy-eyed and listless all morning, suddenly roused herself from her torpor at this remark.

'The man *you* dragged *me* apart from all my friends to get away from, you mean,' she said.

'If you're worried that this man might be a danger to you, Dawn, then we can slap an injunction on him to prevent him from coming near your home,' Gail said.

'A danger? Wayne? He's a pussycat,' Gemma said. 'It's just that when you're a *free spirit*, words like *commitment* make my mother feel a bit queasy.'

Dawn slid a cigarette between her glossed lips and lit it, pointedly ignoring the implied criticism in Gemma's words.

'That's when she stuck a pin in a map and decided it was time to leave Manchester and come and live here,' Gemma added.

Gail quickly worked out that just another half a centimetre and they'd have ended up in the North Sea.

Dawn blew out her match and inhaled deeply.

'Who needs a man like that anyway?' she said. 'Working for peanuts every hour God sends.'

This brief verbal exchange had obviously exhausted Gemma, who rose from her seat, slunk over to the window and fixed her desperate eyes on some indeterminate spot on the landscape. Gail felt desperately sorry for her. If she could have conjured up her lost baby there and then, she would have.

Suddenly Gemma let out a shriek. Gail was on her feet immediately and by her side, hope bubbling up inside her that, finally, here was someone with good news about Justin.

Loitering by the gate, perhaps uncertain this was the house he wanted, stood a youth, indistinguishable to Gail in his hoodie, jeans and trainers from countless others who lived on this estate. But not, apparently, to Gemma, who, trembling, shrank back from the window.

'What's the matter, Gemma?' Gail laid a reassuring hand on her shoulder.

'It's Paul,' she said, her voice shaking.

'What the..!'

Dawn was out of her seat, out of the front door and down the path in a trice. She could get up when she wanted to, then, Gail was relieved to note, as she braced herself to jump in if things got rowdy.

The youth — admirably, Gail thought — seemed to be dealing with an agitated

Dawn quite calmly, ignoring her wrath as if he had absolutely no interest in what she had to say. Mid tirade, he shoved his way past her, marched up the path and strode into the house.

Once inside, he stopped dead in his tracks when he saw a uniformed officer in the room. 'I don't want no trouble,' he said.

'That's good,' Gail said. 'Because neither do I.'

'I just want to know if this is my baby, Gem.'

He fixed his eyes on Gemma pleadingly. She shrank back even further, almost as if she were on the verge of wrapping herself in the curtains for protection.

'You went away,' she said. 'I came to see you. Every day for a week. But you'd gone. No note. No text. Nothing.'

Paul's eyes registered surprise, then incomprehension. Finally, as Dawn stormed back in and shoved past him to lay a protective hand on her daughter, he turned on her, his eyes flashing with rage.

'Ask *her*!' he yelled. 'Ask *her* if I didn't leave no message. *She* said you'd gone back to Manchester.'

Dawn shrugged, as if she hadn't a clue what he was talking about.

'Mum?' Slowly, Gemma began to extricate herself from the curtains. 'I asked you, loads of times. 'You won't see him again,' you said. Why?'

'Why d'you think? He's a waster, like Wayne, like your dad. Men like that — with no money — women are better off without them.'

'I work hard,' Paul said. 'I can make enough money to support my son. And Gemma, if she'll have me.'

Gemma caught her breath. Dawn sent them both a look of disgust, before stamping out of the room. The little house shook as she clattered upstairs, slamming the bedroom door behind her before, finally, peace descended.

'I'll go and put the kettle on, shall I?' Gail said. 'A cup of tea might calm us all down.'

But now that the two of them were wrapped in each other's arms, finally reunited, tea was obviously the last thing on their minds.

★ ★ ★

Katerina Iliescu lay back on her pillow. All she wanted was to be allowed to sleep, but they wouldn't let her. They just kept asking her the same questions, over and over. Did you know your attacker, Katerina? Can you give us his name? And over and over she'd replied that she'd opened the door, a strange man had burst in and attacked her and that was all she remembered. She couldn't betray Valentin. He'd know it was her and then he'd come back. She'd stick to her story, she decided. They'd have to believe her in the end.

'She's lying,' Casey said to PC Tony Lennon, as they left the ward together.

Tony agreed that she was probably protecting someone.

'Yes, and I know who that person is,' Casey said.

Briefly she described the incident earlier, when she'd come across the man she was convinced was Katerina's attacker at reception here in the hospital, demanding to see her.

'I was too nice to him,' she said. 'I should have played Alpha dog. Barked loudly right away, so he wouldn't dare start anything. It's obvious he's waited for her to get back home, then done this to her.'

'Have we got a name for this guy?'

Casey shook her head. 'But I know where he works,' she said. 'He's a bouncer at La Copa.'

Tony gave a long, low whistle.

'Blimey, I think I know the one you mean. Foreign accent. Looks like Pluto?'

An accurate enough description, Casey agreed.

'Well, if you think you're going there alone, you've another think coming,' Tony said.

Casey bristled. 'Meaning?' she snapped.

Had Tony discovered her secret? She'd wanted to keep her pregnancy quiet for a bit longer. There'd been the incident with the coffee, earlier, when she'd said if it was all the same to him she'd prefer tea. That might have put him on to it, since Casey was renowned for her coffee consumption.

'Don't take offence! I just mean that it'd take two of us to take that one down, so I think I should come with you.'

'That's what I thought you meant,' she said, relieved.

On the way to La Copa, they discussed Katerina's condition further. She looked a mess, but the cuts to her face and the bruising to her ribs were superficial.

'Control say the call for an ambulance was made by a man. I wonder who he was and why he didn't hang around till it arrived? There's something definitely going on here I wouldn't mind getting to the bottom of,' Casey said.

'They said he had an English accent, so it couldn't have been her attacker in a fit of remorse,' Tony said. 'Men like him should be put away for a long time,'

'Trouble is, Tony,' Casey replied, as they drew up outside the bar, 'as long as there's women like Katerina Iliescu around to protect them, they never will be.'

★ ★ ★

It was quiet at La Copa, the place only really coming into its own round about eight in the evening, when it suddenly began to fill up, getting steadily busier as the night wore on.

'The boss is in the back,' a young, cheerful-looking bartender, quartering limes at a speed of knots and tossing them into a glass bowl, said. 'Bit — er — tied up at the moment. But I'll get him for you, if you like.'

'What about your bouncer? Is he here?' Tony asked.

'Don't think Valentin's in till the weekend.'

Just then, Graham Marchbank came into the bar from out the back, carrying what Casey at first thought was a bundle of tea towels. When the towels began to wriggle slightly in Graham's arms and emit a kind of gurgling sound, she realised exactly how wrong she'd been.

Graham Marchbank's mouth dropped open when he saw who his visitor was and he hugged the bundle closer.

'Boss, I told you, I'm not serving that baby. No ID, no alcohol, sonny,' the bartender quipped.

Graham Marchbank relaxed a little.

'The wife,' he said, by way of explanation. 'She has to be somewhere. I said I'd take him for a couple of hours.'

'Let's hope you don't get a rush on, then, sir,' Casey said.

'Is this about the robbery?'

Marchbank dipped his head forward to dab away the beads of sweat forming on his brow. He'd not been exactly welcoming the last time she'd been here, but now he looked positively terrified. What was making him sweat so much? she wondered.

The more she came into contact with this man, the less she trusted him. If things hadn't been as they were — the missing baby and now this thug on the loose, Casey would have arrested him right away, taken him back to the station, baby or no baby, and grilled him till she discovered exactly what he was keeping from her about the theft of thousands of pounds from his night safe.

When she mentioned the nature of their visit, he cowered slightly.

'Valentin? I don't know if I have an address for him,' he said. 'He works here on a casual basis and I pay him cash in hand.'

'Did he have references when he came to work for you?' Tony asked. 'And where's he from exactly?'

'I — no — he just turned up one day — we'd had some trouble. Said he was from Romania, I think. Look, what exactly has he done?'

The baby, invisible but for its thick black thatch of hair, wriggled more strenuously. Marchbank jiggled him in his arms, shushing him all the while.

Tony explained, graphically, exactly what Valentin had done. Marchbank's face fell as he took it in.

'Do you know this girl, Mr Marchbank?' Casey asked him. 'I mean, did he ever mention he had a girlfriend?'

'Look, I don't know anything. Not where he lives, not who his girlfriend is. Nothing.' The baby squawked. 'You can see how I'm fixed. If you don't mind I'm going to have to take Georgie back home. It's obvious he can't stay here much longer.'

Tentatively, Casey put out her hand and stroked the baby's head.

'Georgie,' she murmured. 'Nice name. How old is he?'

'About a couple of weeks, that's all,' Marchbank replied through tight lips.

'Never even told us the missis was pregnant,' the bartender put in.

Tony sighed. 'Much as I'd like to stay here and banter . . . '

He cast a meaningful look at Casey. Reluctantly, she removed her hand from the baby's silky head. She was doing it again and this time Tony definitely *had* spotted it.

'You're right, officer,' she said. Turning to Marchbank, she added, 'If we can't get an address from you, we'll have to try other means.'

Casey didn't think she was imagining the fear in Marchbank's eyes.

★　★　★

It took hardly any time at all to find out everything they needed to know about Valentin from a very helpful Police Department in

75

Bucharest. Valentin Sebastian Basescu had a string of offences behind him, all violent and many connected with blackmail. He didn't discriminate either and was just as happy to use his fists on a woman as on a man. Currently he was wanted for at least three violent offences, having skipped bail a few months previously and, slipping through the net of passport control, escaped to the UK.

'What's Valentin got on Katerina, do you think?' Tony Lennon said.

'There's only one way to find out,' Casey said. 'If she didn't talk last time it was because she hadn't seen what he was capable of. But once I show her these . . . '

Snatching up the digital photos of three of Valentin's badly beaten victims, she ordered Tony to drive the car round to the front of the station, while she made a quick check on what — if any — progress had been made in the search for baby Justin.

It was as she'd thought. He'd been spotted in places as far apart as Land's End and John O'Groats. He'd been seen with a woman; with two women; with a couple. On and on went the variations. None of them carrying even the slightest grain of truth, probably.

A message on her phone from Gail told her Gemma's boyfriend was back and that although Dawn was unhappy about this, Gemma was delighted. Casey just had time to make a quick call and ask Gail one vital question, then she'd feel a lot more confident about cracking the case of the missing baby and discovering the connection between Katerina, Marchbank and Valentin.

* * *

They were on their way back to La Copa, Tony driving at a furious lick

'It's all so blindingly obvious,' she said. 'Why didn't I realise that the baby Marchbank was holding in his arms was Justin?'

'Oldest trick in the book,' Tony said, eyes straight ahead. 'Put the stolen goods right under the detective's nose and they won't spot it. Ask Agatha Christie.'

Casey grinned.

'It was when I asked Marchbank how old his baby was. About a couple of weeks, he said, remember?'

Tony nodded.

'When I rang Gail later, I asked her the same question. How old's your baby, Gail? Know what she said?'

'Go on. Enlighten me.'

'Four months, three weeks and two days.'

'Your point being?'

Tony was forced to slow down now they'd hit the high street.

'During that first year, parents count every day of their baby's life, because every day is a blessing. That's what Gail said. Sounds right, doesn't it?'

Tony nodded grudgingly.

'About two weeks just doesn't sound right, even to someone childless like me.'

Without taking his eyes off the road, Tony said, 'That's your story and you're sticking to it, is it?'

They were outside La Copa now. Casey pursed her lips.

'Haven't a clue what you're talking about, Tony,' she said. 'But if you breathe one word . . .'

'My lips are sealed, guv,' Tony said. 'But congratulations, anyway. Now, we've got a job to do.'

★ ★ ★

A distraught Katerina had pleaded with Casey to be dealt with leniently. What she'd done was an unforgivable crime. But she hadn't had a moment's peace since she'd committed it, she said.

Valentin had given her no choice. Back home, in Bucharest, she'd blown the whistle at the maternity hospital where she'd worked as a midwife. Three new-born babies had died within a month. The management tried to talk themselves out of it, but Katerina, who for a long time had been appalled by the poor hygiene procedures carried out at the hospital, had finally spoken to the Press.

There'd been an outcry. The whole of the management team were sacked, but not before they'd got rid of Katerina. She'd left in disgrace without references and Valentin, whom she'd met here in Brockhaven, came to her rescue, creating glowing testimonials for her which enabled her to get the job of nursery nurse at Brockhaven General.

But getting her to snatch a baby to help out a friend of his was payback time. She'd made the huge error of taking an infant with an easily identifiable birthmark.

When the woman — Katerina knew her only as Valentin's boss's wife — realised that the baby hadn't come from Romania at all, as she'd been told, she wanted to give the baby back. It was when a distraught Graham Marchbank had relayed this information to Valentin that Valentin had visited her at home and beaten her up for her carelessness.

While Casey and Tony had been interviewing Katerina, Valentin had been caught. On learning he was about to be repatriated, he'd decided he might as well be hung for a sheep as for a lamb and came clean about his part in the robbery at La Copa. Katerina had known nothing of it, and had categorically received no money from it either, he said.

Marchbank was the only piece missing

for the jigsaw to be complete. 'The one thing you have in your favour, Graham,' Casey said, taking the baby from him, 'is that you rang for the ambulance for Katerina.'

At the mention of her name, Graham's eyes lit up. Would it be all right if he visited her in hospital, he asked? Casey didn't enjoy telling him she doubted he'd get bail. Robbing his own safe was bad enough, with the waste of police time it had incurred. But the second crime . . . Maybe one day they could meet again, and then who knew what might happen?

'Promise me you'll get some help for Vanessa, Inspector,' he said, as she led him out to the car. 'I did this for her, you know. So we could be happy. But it's too late for that now. It's been too late for a long time.'

Maybe it was her hormones, but she couldn't help feeling the tiniest bit of sympathy for this basically good man who'd done bad things.

Casey's hormones were clearly working overtime that day. That was the only explanation she could find for the lump in her throat, as she watched a beaming Gemma Stebbings take her baby in her arms, tears of relief and joy shining in her eyes.

The tiny living room was full to bursting now she and PC Tony Lennon had turned up to add to the numbers. Soon, when word got round, the Press and local TV would be here, too. But for Gemma, Casey guessed, the room was empty, apart from the two people who meant most to her.

On the settee, Gemma sat with boyfriend, Paul, whose face was lit up with pride. Her eyes were fixed hungrily on Justin, as if she still didn't trust herself to believe he'd been returned to her unscathed. Now, as she buried her face in Justin's tummy, or tweaked his tiny nose playfully, her youth and vitality reappeared as if by magic and Casey marvelled at the change in her.

'Our work here is done,' she muttered to Gail and Tony, who were gawping just as besottedly as she was, she was relieved to see.

Four months later, Casey and Dom, arm in arm, were taking a stroll along the prom. Casey was thinking of very little other than the necessity of an ice cream and soon, so was startled when someone stopped her and said hello.

At first, she failed to recognise the woman, arm in arm with a tall, dreadlocked black guy.

'It's me, Dawn Stebbings. Remember? And this is Wayne. Couldn't get rid of him. He's a permanent fixture now, but perhaps it's just as well.'

Paul patted Dawn's tummy proprietorially.

'Snap!' Dawn said, pointing at Casey's own small bump.

Casey blushed. Looking past Dawn, she spotted a young couple behind them — it was Gemma — a prettier, more relaxed Gemma — and the prodigal boyfriend, Paul, proudly pushing baby Justin, unrecognisable from the newborn he'd been when last she'd seen him.

They chatted for a while, Casey and

Dom heaping compliments on Justin's progress to the proud parents. Dawn's invitation came out of the blue just as they were about to part. There was to be a double wedding — Wayne and herself; Gemma and Paul.

'You must both come,' Dawn insisted. 'After everything you did to get Justin back.'

Gemma agreed, with an enthusiasm Casey had never witnessed in her before.

'Provided you're not otherwise engaged by then?' Dawn added, with a nod at Casey's bump.

In the end, there was no reason to say no.

'Happy families at last,' Casey said.

'I've always thought,' Dom said, 'that if you were going to get married, then September would be the best month for it.' Taking Casey's hand, he added. 'How about you?'

In at the Deep End

1

The invitation, propped up on the mantelpiece, had arrived three days ago, yet still remained unanswered. 'I don't mind if you go,' Dom said. 'You'll enjoy seeing Eleanor again.' Framed in the doorway, he screwed up his eyes against the midday glare. It really was time they thought about getting curtains up at the window. After all, they'd been in the new house for a month now.

'But there's so much to do.' Casey swept her arm around the spacious, still sparsely furnished room. How on earth she'd managed to make Detective Inspector so quickly, when she couldn't even decide what kind of flooring she wanted, or even whether or not to accept her friend's invitation to attend the opening of the new pool at the college where she was a Senior Fellow, was a miracle. Not that Dom was any more decisive than she was. Hotshot journalist on a top London newspaper, working from a laptop in his office, aka the kitchen table.

'Put me in charge, if you're really not bothered about what goes on the floor or the windows.'

Truly she wasn't (as long as it wasn't beige). She was a career woman. Except now she was meant to be taking it easy.

'OK,' she said.

Dom crossed the room and encircled her mummy tummy with his embrace.

'A change is as good as a rest, Mother,' he said, in a very bad Northern accent. 'And at Doughty Hall, I can guarantee you'll get both.'

★　★　★

The casual workers might think it was perfectly acceptable only to half-listen with glazed eyes while Naomi Dodd gave her pep talk, but as Bursar of Doughty Hall, Naomi didn't. *And* she'd seen that Josh Hathaway nudging the Polish girl, Danuta, at something she'd said that he'd no doubt found an innuendo in. No skin off his nose if they ran out of glasses at tomorrow's big do, was it? Come the end of the shift, he'd still get his money.

At least Danuta knew enough to keep her eyes forward and her face straight, no matter how often he nudged her. But then Danuta's mother wasn't Lady Violet Hathaway, Dean of Doughty Hall, was she? Danuta needed to hang on to this job for a good deal longer than it would take Josh to scrape enough together for a plane ticket to Australia or wherever the clever little creep was heading off to on his gap year. Blocking Josh from her eye line as much as she could, she continued.

'Remember to be professional at all times. Make sure your uniforms are spotless and that your nails are clean. Oh, and smile.'

There was more shuffling and coughing, accompanied by a show of badly concealed yawns. What was wrong with them? Susannah Storey was coming here tomorrow to open the pool. *The* Susannah Storey. There was to be a ceremony, dignitaries, a buffet, the works.

One of Susannah Storey's novels was bought every thirty seconds at airports around the world, she'd discovered only last week. A snippet that hadn't impressed her staff one jot when she'd shared it at the start of the briefing.

'OK, I'm off now,' she said, reaching for her checklist. 'You know where I am if you want me.'

She was at the door, her mind already set on the next thing, when Danuta came running after her, holding out her bag.

'You forgot this, Naomi.'

Danuta's smile was timid and her voice soft. She didn't want to be accused of creeping.

'Second time this morning,' she added. 'Forget my head if it wasn't screwed on!'

Naomi rolled her eyes in self-mockery, practically snatching the bag from Danuta before scurrying away to her office. This wasn't the exit she'd envisaged. It made her appear daffy and ineffectual. On top of this, she'd heard the collective sigh of relief that had greeted her departure, and it stung.

'Teacher's pet,' Josh said, catching Danuta's eye.

Danuta blushed. She always blushed when Josh spoke to her. Sometimes she even blushed when all he did was look at her. He strolled towards her, his gait loose-limbed, his hands shoved casually in the pockets of his white coat. He should have had his hair covered. Naomi must have seen, but she hadn't pointed it out. Josh could get away with murder, she'd heard it said when she'd first arrived at Doughty Hall, and she could well believe it.

'Come outside and have a smoke with me now she's gone.'

Danuta had a stack of cutlery to polish and Josh had been told to make sure the stockpot had been scoured before he went off shift. What was he playing at?

'You know I don't smoke,' she said, pushing his arm away so she could get to the drawer.

'Come and watch me smoke, then.'

'I know about your smoking. I know what a spliff smells like.'

Josh's expression was one of mock horror.

'What are you suggesting? Or is it

Naomi Dodd you're worried about?' He pitched his voice high and transformed his face, so he looked more than a little crazy. '*It was my idea to ask Susannah Storey down here to her old college to open the new swimming pool. If anything goes wrong I'll kill myself.*'

Danuta couldn't help laughing. 'That's her to a T. But it is a lot of responsibility for her. Like she said, she had a fight with some of the Fellows about asking a writer of pulp fiction down to perform the ceremony.'

'My mother only reads books in Latin and Greek, so it's not surprising.' Josh sneered.

Always this sneer when he mentioned his mother's name. There was no closeness between Josh and his mother at all. He'd made that plain enough the day he'd caught Danuta crying over a letter from Poland. Just hearing from her mum made her so homesick, she'd confided. He'd tried to sympathise but it was clear he just didn't get how anybody could possess such strong feelings for their family.

He had been scrabbling in the cup-board for some time. With a flourish, he handed her a pink cloth and a small tin of polish.

'Voila!' He made a sweeping bow. 'Obviously not taking her medication,' he added.

'You think so?'

Maybe Naomi *had* been a little hyper today. In and out the kitchen, losing lists, forgetting where she put her bag. But medication?

'A joke, Danuta. Don't take everything so seriously!'

Danuta snatched the cloth and tin from him. 'Go and have your smoke and let me get on with my work.'

He went, not even bothering to check if Chef had spotted him skiving. Such a nerve! It wasn't the first time Danuta had asked herself why Josh was skivvying in the kitchen of the prestigious university college where his mother was Dean. She knew that his father had died when he was a little boy, and that he'd never really known him either, because, for the best part of Josh's life, he'd been an invalid.

But even as a widow his mother must be earning three times the combined salary of her own parents. Why didn't she just write him a cheque instead of making him scrub pans and wash dishes? She'd never understand the English and their strange ways, she decided, picking up another knife.

★   ★   ★

Lady Violet Hathaway took a sip from her second large glass of whisky of the evening and lay back in her armchair, waiting for it to weave its magic. It had been another busy day, but the prospect of being able to wind down now that it was Friday evening was doomed, thanks to the wretched pool-opening ceremony tomorrow afternoon.

If she hadn't already been so exhausted by Josh's antics, she'd have put up more of a fight against Naomi Dodd and her crackpot idea of inviting Susannah Storey up to cut the ribbon. God only knew, there were far more suitable alumni! Susannah had been her tutee when she was up at Doughty twenty years ago and had made little impression on her at the time. Since she'd left the literary agency, where she'd gone straight from getting her rather poor second, and started writing trashy novels, she'd made even less of one.

But Naomi Dodd had been on some sort of Susannah crusade. Nobody else could get the college the same sort of publicity, she'd insisted. On and on for weeks. In the end, she'd worn her down.

Funny, but at her interview she hadn't thought Naomi Dodd was the type to get the bit between her teeth about anything very much, which was partly why she'd taken her on in the first place. There were enough strong-willed people at Doughty Hall to contend with, frankly. Naomi had come over as a pleasant, if rather apologetic woman, maybe a tad irritating in her enthusiasm, others on the selection panel had suggested, but Lady Violet, the most strong-willed of all, had stood her ground.

The other reason she'd wanted to offer Naomi the job was that she'd felt sorry for her. She hadn't dwelled on her situation, but Lady Violet had gleaned enough to learn she'd lost a fiancé in such tragic circumstances that it had tipped her over into a nervous breakdown and that this was the first job she'd applied for since she'd been signed off by her doctor. Everyone deserves a second chance, she'd insisted, and before this episode in her life her CV had been exemplary. The panel had to agree. She'd hired her on the spot.

But maybe the others were right and she'd let her feelings cloud her judgment. She took another sip of her whisky, then reached for her remote control and turned the TV on. The great soporific — better even than whisky. It would take her mind off everything. Naomi Dodd, Susannah Storey, Josh. No, not Josh. He was never far from her thoughts.

It was Josh who'd made the rather cruel and — to her mind — completely inaccurate comment that it was always much easier for her to give the benefit of the doubt to strangers than to members of her own family. Nineteen years old, that's all he was, and already such an embittered young man. Where had he got the idea that the world owed him a living? Not from her, certainly, and not even from his father, whom Josh had barely known. Unless, contrary to popular belief, nature exerted more influence than nurture after all and he'd simply inherited the characteristic along with his father's dark curls and cruel, grey eyes.

No, she didn't enjoy having him at such close quarters. But the job of potman had come up and he'd needed the money, and she'd had no intention of giving him any more of hers. She wouldn't support his drugs habit and she wouldn't finance a trip to Australia either.

For once, he'd bitten the bullet. She had too much on him this time, pinching from her purse. And then he'd been caught red-handed pilfering from a colleague! He'd come within an inch of being reported to the police and it had pulled him up sharp.

The television suddenly caught Lady Violet's attention.

'And now, another whose novels you can't fail to have seen piled high at bookshops everywhere. Susannah Storey talks to me about her latest, *Never Too*

Late, a stylish romp that charts the highs and lows of feisty anti-heroine, Dolores Dervish.'

Lady Violet groped for the remote that had slipped down the side of the chair and turned up the volume. This she *had* to see! There was Susannah, relaxed and exuding confidence, smiling a cosmetically enhanced smile, her hair far blonder and glossier than ever it had been when she'd been an undergraduate. In fact, she was barely recognisable as the pasty-faced, skinny student she'd once been; the girl who would speak into her chest and rarely raise her eyes, unless it was to stumble over an apology for being late with an essay.

As she sipped her way to the bottom of the glass, Lady Violet gleaned that Susannah preferred to write longhand, that she only went to a computer for the final draft, that she took her manuscript with her whenever she spent the night away from her north London town house, and that she showed no one, not even her agent, what she was writing until it was typed up and complete.

'So you're not going to give us any titbits about your work in progress, then?' The interviewer leaned forward, tense with hope.

'All I can say,' Susannah said coyly, 'is that the book I'm writing at the moment is based on a real incident.'

'Oh?' Expectation hovered on the interviewer's face.

'I haven't quite settled on the title but I rather like the sound of *Town And Gown*, because it deals with a scandal that happened at my old college, involving a senior figure and a member of the public.' Then she let out a peal of laughter. 'That's all I'm saying for now, though. I haven't quite finished it and I don't want to jinx it by giving too much away!'

Lady Violet's scalp began to prickle. A chill ran through her, despite the warming whisky. No. She couldn't be thinking of dragging up all that business again, surely?

★　★　★

Casey helped herself to another canapé. Her lower back was beginning to ache and she wasn't sure how much longer she could stand. Because the food, such as it was, had been set out on raised benches around the newly opened pool, it left very little room for seating. Most people stood around in small groups, their conversation — lubricated by glasses of cava, topped up at regular intervals by politely smiling college staff — echoing loudly around the new building. Rocking on her heels to relieve the pressure on her back, she surveyed the scene. Central to it, of course, was Susannah Storey, glossy in an airbrushed magazine cover kind of way that didn't come cheap, while she accepted compliments with well-rehearsed grace.

'Isn't she just wonderful?' cooed the Bursar, to whom she'd been introduced some fifteen minutes previously by Eleanor, who'd cleverly sneaked off to refill her glass and hadn't yet returned. Casey didn't think she ever would. This was her fate, she decided, to be stuck in this *Groundhog Day* conversation with Naomi Dodd, a large woman clad in a flower-sprigged dress that would have been perfect on a woman three sizes smaller and fifteen years younger. How many times had she let

Casey know just what a big fan she was of Susannah Storey, and what a coup it had been for her to persuade her to return to her alma mater to cut the ribbon at the opening of the new pool?

Casey longed to make her excuses. Eleanor and she were both staying in college for the night, in adjacent rooms. 'So you can get the whole college experience, dear, and not have to put up with dreary old me for the entire weekend,' was how Eleanor had explained it. Casey hadn't had the heart to tell her that, these days, she was usually in bed by nine and that her idea of living it up was a lime-and-lemonade at The Anchor, followed by the short walk back home.

It was easy enough to keep up the pretence of listening. Naomi, mid-flow, had a habit of tilting her head to one side and closing her eyes as she spoke. All Casey had to do to maintain the fiction that she was listening intently was to nod and smile as soon as Naomi re-opened her eyes.

She'd managed to spot one or two interesting things by applying this trick. One of the waiters, a young man, hair scraped back in a kind of ponytail, sneaking a glass of cava when he thought no one was looking, for one. She recognised him as the cocky type. Thought he was smart, but what he hadn't realised was that he'd been spotted not just by her but by one of the other waiters — a young, pretty girl with huge eyes and a perfect oval face.

Casey watched her follow the boy round the room with her eyes, constantly checking up on his whereabouts. Was she in charge here? Or was it more personal? Hmm, interesting, but from the smoke rising in her eyes, Casey would lay odds that this young man was in for a roasting as soon as they got back to the kitchen.

Then there was the restrained exchange she witnessed between the Dean and Susannah Storey. It may have been Lady Violet's college, but it was obvious, from Susannah's smug look, that whatever their conversation was about, it was the writer not the academic who had the upper hand. What was all that about? she wondered.

A waiter approached, touching Naomi's elbow. She excused herself with a squeak and Casey, suppressing a sigh of relief, took the opportunity to head for her room, informing Eleanor, who she spotted on the way in conversation with the news reporter, where she was going.

Her room was small yet functional. Removing her shoes, but too exhausted to think about rummaging in her overnight bag for her nightie, Casey flopped down on the narrow bed. Ten o'clock. A late night for her, was her last thought, before she drifted off to sleep.

She didn't know what had woken her. The baby, probably, shifting in her womb, trying to find a more comfortable position. The room was pitch-black, the only light the glare from her watch. One-thirty, it said. Casey made several attempts to find a more comfortable position herself. It was a precarious business in this narrow bed and, now fully awake, she gave it up as a bad job. Her back was still niggling and the only thing that would stop it was a walk. Or better still a swim. Hadn't Lady Violet insisted she use the pool whenever she felt like it? That she herself had found swimming beneficial in her own late pregnancy? Well, maybe she hadn't meant at one-thirty in the morning, but, why not? she mused, glad she'd taken Dom's advice and packed her maternity costume.

There was no one around as she made her way silently towards the pool. Everyone at Doughty Hall, apparently, kept to a conservative routine. Only the moon lit up her route. There were two entrances to the pool, she remembered — presumably hierarchical. She had no idea if the door she'd chosen was for staff or students, but there was no one here to tell her off if she was breaking protocol. Only then did it occur to her it might be locked, which would be a huge pity.

From the other side of the pine, panelled door came a sudden shriek, and then another and another. Footsteps thundered towards her, accompanied by the sound of panting breath. Casey jumped aside as the wooden door flew open. She recognised the girl from earlier — the waitress with the oval face and beautiful eyes. Now her eyes were wild, her face distorted. Casey pushed past her.

It was the sheets of paper she noticed first, floating on top of the pool, running with ink, indecipherable now. But she knew there was more. The girl's screams had warned her of it. Down, down, down she stared, shading her eyes against the glare of the pool lights. And then she saw it. The body. Susannah Storey. Dead.

★　★　★

Breakfast was rather a scrappy affair at Doughty Hall the morning after the body of the best-selling author had been discovered at the bottom of the college's brand-new pool, surrounded by several hundred completely sodden pages of her yet-to-be-delivered manuscript.

'Hardly surprising,' remarked Dr Eleanor Humphreys, peering over her cup of tea through round-rimmed spectacles, 'since one of the best waitresses is currently being interviewed by the police.'

Casey, bleary-eyed, watched her friend struggle with a miniature pot of jam. She'd come to Doughty Hall for a change but the weekend was fast turning into a busman's holiday. Finding the body had been a shock. Had the shock been just as great for Danuta, the Polish waitress, who'd almost knocked her flying as she'd come running hell for leather away from the pool? Or was the fainting fit that followed her wild shrieks just an act? Was Danuta a killer, or simply an unfortunate witness, as she herself had been?

'What do you know about this Danuta Brodsky, Eleanor? Is she a killer, do you think?'

'Don't you think — in your condition — that you should leave this investigation to the local police? Let *them* get to the bottom of it.'

Casey hated to speak ill of her colleagues, but she'd met DI John McGrath before, and frankly, didn't think much of his methods.

'Tell me about Danuta,' she said.

'She's lovely. A good worker, keen to learn English. I even wrote her a pass, so she could have access to the library to use the computers there, to help her study.'

'But?'

'Well, if you put it like that,' she said, 'the 'but' is Josh Hathaway.'

Casey gave a start. 'Hathaway? Isn't

that the Dean's name?'

'Josh is her son. On his gap year. He's working in the kitchens, washing dishes.'

Ah! The good-looking one with the attitude she'd seen swigging the leftover cava at the reception yesterday. Her instinct had been right. These two youngsters were in some sort of relationship.

'You don't approve, then?'

Eleanor pursed her lips. 'I'm afraid he may be taking advantage of her — a young girl in a foreign country. I worry that he may try to lead her astray, that's all.'

Casey suppressed a smile. It was at times like this that she remembered the gap in their ages. In Eleanor's day, being single usually meant leading a chaste existence. But how much would Danuta Brodsky, who'd left her country to explore life in another, worry about being taken advantage of? Particularly by someone as physically attractive as Josh Hathaway.

* * *

In the kitchen, Josh lounged by the window, observing the arrival of more police and forensic specialists. Just as keenly, Danuta observed him from the doorway, unable to decide if it was herself or Josh she was more angry with. She'd made a fool of herself in her interview with the Detective Inspector.

If they didn't arrest her for murder before the day was out, it would be a miracle.

At that moment, Josh turned round. His face lit up when he saw her. If only he wasn't so good-looking, Danuta thought, then none of this would have happened.

'Hey. They didn't put the cuffs on you, then.'

'Be quiet, Josh,' she snapped. 'I've got a headache. And it's your fault. I've spent the last half-hour being interrogated.'

Josh gave a low whistle. 'Big word,' he said. 'Your English is really coming on.'

'Oh, shut up and get me a glass of water.'

'You're so attractive when you're angry,' Josh teased.

He was making no effort to do what she'd asked, so she stomped over to the sink, grabbed a glass en route, then filled it to the brim.

'What did he ask you?'

Danuta drained the glass, aware that all the while Josh's eyes were on her.

'He asked me what I was doing at the swimming pool at that hour, of course, what do you think?'

'Did you tell him the truth?'

She glared at him and slammed the glass down so hard on the draining board it shattered.

'What a pity.' Her tone was sarcastic. 'We really are getting very short of glasses, aren't we, Josh?'

There was a momentary flicker of discomfort in Josh's eyes. It made her feel powerful. Right now she knew something he didn't and Josh clearly disliked the role reversal.

When she'd told the Inspector she'd returned to the pool at such a late hour, because she needed to check that all the glasses that had been used at the reception had been returned, she'd failed to anticipate his next question.

'And had they?' he'd asked her.

She hadn't liked the look of this policeman, his forehead all shiny with sweat. All she needed to say was 'yes'. But instead she'd stumbled over her answer and ended up saying nothing. Now she told Josh what she failed to tell the policeman.

'These crystal glasses — the best ones, kept for VIPs. I saw you wheel them over to the pool on the trolley in the afternoon. I told you to bring them back to the kitchen after the reception was over. They weren't where they should have been at ten o'clock last night. I couldn't sleep, worrying I would get the blame if they'd gone missing. That's why I went back. I hoped they'd be there and you'd just forgotten to bring them back.'

'Not to kill Susannah Storey, then?'

Josh was making fun of her again. Her moment of power had evaporated. She hated him.

'I should have told the policeman you stole them,' she snapped. 'No doubt you gave them to your dealer in exchange for drugs.'

Josh yawned and stretched. 'You take this job far too seriously, Danuta,' he said. 'It's really not worth losing sleep over stuff going missing when it doesn't even belong to you.'

'You don't even bother to deny it,' she said.

He shrugged. 'Like anybody's going to be worrying about a few glasses when there's a murderer on the loose. I mean, seriously.'

Why had she bothered to protect him? Now the inspector thought she was hiding something even bigger than stolen glasses from him.

'What about Naomi?'

Josh gave a start.

'Has she missed her purse yet, do you think?'

'I know how I might look to you, Danuta, but honestly — if you knew how tight my mother was. I took the glasses to spite her, I admit it. She could buy another set tomorrow if she felt like it, out of her own money. But Naomi's purse . . . '

He shook his head, bewildered. 'I'm sorry, you've lost me.' Then his face cleared. 'Wait a minute. Yes, you're right. I did pick up her bag. It was under one of the benches round the pool. I swept it into a bin liner for a laugh. You know how she's always leaving it lying around then walking off and forgetting all about it.'

Danuta said nothing.

'It was a joke, Danuta. You don't think I stole it, did you? I gave it back to her later when I realised she hadn't even missed it. You can ask her if you like.'

'No, I don't need to do that.'

It was clever of him to challenge her like that. Of course she wouldn't ask Naomi if she'd missed her purse.

'You do believe me, then? Because it's the truth I'm telling you.'

'Of course I believe you, Josh. But I'm tired now. If you don't mind, I'm going to my room to sleep a couple of hours before I start work again.'

She needed to get away. He was wired with nervous energy, like a cat about to pounce. She shouldn't have crossed him — but if she hadn't, she'd never have discovered what he was really like.

2

DI John McGrath, in his shiny suit, looked out of place in the elegant, high-ceilinged Fellows' library that the Dean had insisted he use as an interview room. Casey had come across him before and didn't like his methods. McGrath and his sort were a dying breed — slow to act and quick to take the credit.

Meanwhile, she had plenty to think about, now she knew that Forensics had discovered cuts to the side of Storey's head and contusions to the brain. That she had drowned was a fact, but what happened first was still under investigation. The empty wine bottle she'd been struck with had been discovered in the water with her, alongside the pages of her manuscript — none of which could now be deciphered, thanks to the chlorine that had bleached the ink — so any fingerprints or DNA had been deleted.

'So what now?' she asked McGrath.

'We'll carry on interviewing everyone present in college last night, and trawling through CCTV.'

At that moment, the phone on McGrath's desk burst into shrill life. When he put it down, he positively pulsated with energy.

'One of my lads has just interviewed a Mrs Deborah Pullen, who witnessed an argument at a bus shelter in town yesterday lunchtime between the victim and a youth. They're already checking CCTV at the spot the incident occurred. I'd like to hear her story for myself. Come along if you're not too tired,' he said, with a glance at her bump.

'I think I'll manage,' Casey said sweetly, the smile nearly choking her as she followed him to his car.

★ ★ ★

'So, Mrs Pullen, tell me what happened yesterday.'

'There were three of us in the bus shelter, besides him. Before *she* came along, I mean. We were all waiting for the number sixteen. I know that goes to Doughty Hall, because my neighbour's a cleaner there and it's the one she catches. When it turns up, that is.'

Casey wondered what Susannah Storey was doing catching a bus.

'Anyway, where was I?'

McGrath reminded her and soon she was back in full flow.

'There was this lad, see, smoking. In the shelter. None of us said nothing, because — well, you don't like to, do you, these days?'

At this point, she changed her voice into a passable imitation of Susannah Storey.

''Do you realise it's against the law to smoke here?' she asked him. He didn't like it one bit. Language I wouldn't like to repeat.'

'And what was Miss Storey's reaction?'

'She smiled at him, like it had all just washed over her. 'Course, that made him worse. He had another rant then.'

'Did you at any time think he might attack Miss Storey, Mrs Pullen?'

'Oh, yes. He was having a right tantrum.'

'So how did this all end, Mrs Pullen?'

There was a knock on the door. A flicker of irritation at the interruption spread over John McGrath's face. Casey slid out of he chair and went to open it, silencing the young officer with a look, as she took half a dozen still printouts of the CCTV at the bus stop.

'Flicked his lit cigarette at her, then went stomping off. I was glad to see the back of him.'

Casey stared first at one picture, then at the rest.

Slowly, she walked back to the desk and laid out the pictures like a hand of cards.

'Josh Hathaway,' she said. 'Shifty sort. Dean's son. Lives and works at Doughty Hall.'

'Well, well, what a coincidence,' said McGrath, rubbing his hands together gleefully. 'I think we should bring him in, don't you?'

★ ★ ★

In the police interview room, Josh Hathaway was so relaxed as he flicked through still after still of the scene at the bus shelter that he was almost comatose.

'Thing is,' he said, 'that *is* me. Can't deny it since it's there in black and white. But I don't really remember the incident, officer. You see, I'd had a smoke and it plays havoc with the old memory cells.'

'Didn't you recognise the woman at the bus stop, Josh, when you met her later at Doughty Hall?' Casey asked him.

'To be honest, women over the age of about twenty-five don't really show up on my radar.'

McGrath leaned in close to his quarry, hoping the boy might find his proximity threatening.

'Where were you between eleven last night and one o'clock this morning?'

'Out,' Hathaway said casually. 'And about. You know how it is. Saturday night and all that.'

'You weren't at Doughty Hall, then?'

'On a Saturday night? There's more life in a graveyard.'

'Josh, I really would advise you to be more co-operative,' his solicitor said. 'Just tell them what you told me and then we can all go home.'

'OK,' Josh said, at last. 'I met some friends in The Wishing Well at ten o'clock. We had a few drinks, then walked into town. To Groove.'

'Nightclub in the centre,' McGrath informed Casey.

'Now, why didn't you tell us all that in the beginning?' she said.

'Didn't want to make it too easy for you,' he said, flashing a broad grin.

* * *

Casey took a taxi back to Doughty Hall, having refused a lift from John McGrath. Frankly, she wanted to get as far away from him as possible. He'd got the bit between his teeth as far as Josh Hathaway went, she decided, as the taxi rolled into the college courtyard.

It was a drag having to look through reams of CCTV footage, she agreed, but Susannah Storey was murdered between eleven o'clock on the Saturday night and one o'clock on the Sunday morning. If the footage showed Hathaway grooving away at Groove between those hours, then that was that, and they had better start casting the net elsewhere.

'Casey, I need a word with you in private.'

Eleanor Humphreys had been waiting at the porter's lodge for the taxi to drop her off. She said she'd rung the police station and learned from DI McGrath that Casey had had enough and had gone back to Doughty Hall.

Casey grinned. 'Had enough of *him*,' she said. 'Though I told him I needed to rest my swollen ankles. So, what's up?'

Eleanor's expression was frighteningly serious. 'Come and have a cup of tea in my room and I'll tell you.'

Seated in Eleanor's most comfortable chair, at her insistence, and with her feet up on a velvet footstool, cup of tea in hand, Casey felt ready to hear whatever it was that seemed to be making her friend so anxious.

'I know you've just interviewed Josh Hathaway,' Eleanor said. 'And I'm feeling guilty because I haven't been entirely honest with you about the boy.'

'Oh?'

119

Eleanor wasn't comfortable about revealing something she'd sworn not to, she said, but there were occasions when the truth was more important than a promise.

'Oh, dear. I'm not expressing myself very well, am I?' she said, at Casey's mystified expression. Then, taking a gulp of tea for moral support, she finally blurted it out.

'Last year, Josh Hathaway stole money from me,' she said. 'Lady Violet begged me not to involve the police and, in the end, I agreed not to, though it went against the grain, I can tell you.'

'Was it a lot of money?'

Eleanor shook her head. But it was the principal of the thing, she said. How would Josh ever come to learn the difference between right and wrong, if he was allowed to get away with theft?

'You should talk to his mother, Casey. She's been in the habit of protecting her son since he was a small boy. Maybe this time she's overstepped the mark.'

Casey was puzzled. Surely she didn't believe that Lady Violet would lie about murder?

'Lady Violet has brought up her son single-handedly. Her bond with him is strong.'

'Where's the father in all this, Eleanor?' she asked.

Eleanor shrugged. He'd died when Josh was a young boy, she said, before she'd come to Doughty Hall as a Fellow. She'd never met him personally, although she knew *of* him. Something in the way she phrased her reply alerted Casey.

'Knew *of* him? Did he have some sort of reputation?'

Eleanor fixed Casey with a gimlet eye. 'I'm not in the habit of tittle-tattling, Casey,' she said.

'You're right, Eleanor. It's none of my business,' she said. 'I only hope Lady Violet appreciates your discretion and realises what a good friend she has in you.'

Eleanor's display of authority was over. Leaning forward to pick up the teapot, she smiled. 'I hope so, too,' she said. 'Now, how about another cup of tea?'

★ ★ ★

When Casey was first introduced to Lady Violet Hathaway, her initial impression of the person in charge of Doughty Hall had been of a tall, still-slim woman in late middle-age, with an intelligent face and a rather aristocratic bearing, who long ago had decided on her style and hadn't veered from it since.

But the woman who opened the door of The Lodge to her this evening was very different. Gone were the dark suit, heels and discreet jewellery. In their place, she wore a pair of shabby black trousers and a shapeless sweatshirt that could very well have been one of her son's cast-offs. Her unwashed hair lay flat to her head and she wore no make-up. From her breath, and the high colour in her cheeks, Casey deduced she'd been drinking. The whisky decanter and glass on the polished darkwood table next to her winged chair provided the evidence.

'I've come to see how you are.'

In a glance, Casey took in money and good taste. No wonder Josh felt stifled here, she thought. It would be like living in a museum.

Lady Violet ran her hand through her hair. 'As you see,' she said. 'Not good. I've resorted to the bottle. 'You don't, I suppose.' She gestured towards Casey's bump, before her glance returned longingly to her glass.

'No, but, please. You go ahead.'

'Well, maybe I will have a top-up. Do take a seat, Inspector Clunes.'

She gestured vaguely to the settee.

'You must call me Casey,' she said. 'I'm not really involved in Susannah Storey's case — not officially, anyway. I'm here as a friend, I hope.'

'Well, they're always welcome. Though strangely few and far between since my son's name first came up in connection with *that woman's* unfortunate demise.'

Somewhere in the corner of Casey's mind, a significant memory struggled to get out. Something had occurred at the reception yesterday — something involving Lady Violet and Susannah perhaps?

Her gaze drifted to the impressive fireplace and to the school photo on the mantelpiece. There was Josh, gap-toothed and grinning, neatly dressed in school uniform. He'd have been seven or eight, Casey guessed.

'For what it's worth, Lady Violet,' she said, 'there's absolutely no evidence to connect Josh with Susannah Storey's murder. I've just come from the police station and he left, too, minutes before.'

Relief flooded Lady Violet's face. 'Of course, there's no reason to think he might give his mother a call to let her know he was no longer under suspicion.'

Her words were harsh, but spoken with a mother's fondness.

'It's probably slipped his mind.'

Casey had no intention of correcting Lady Violet in her cheerful assumption that her son was off the hook. After all, there was his alibi to check yet. And there was something else, too. Like a diver splitting the water as he crashed through to the surface, Casey's memory suddenly resurfaced.

'Lady Violet,' she said. 'What were you and Susannah Storey arguing about yesterday at the reception?'

Lady Violet's guard was now up, though she was doing her utmost to conceal it.

'I'm sorry, but I can't recall any argument between Susannah and myself, Inspector.'

It didn't escape Casey's notice that Lady Violet had dropped the 'Casey'. Had she already rehearsed this scenario in anticipation of the incident being raised at some future date — before Casey had been invited into her home and become her new best friend?

She decided to leave it for now. She had her rattled and that was good enough. Let her sleep on it, she mused, as she wished Lady Violet a pleasant good night.

★ ★ ★

Next morning, as Casey made her way out of the dining hall after breakfast, a well-dressed, rather nervous-looking man, dragging a suitcase behind him, stopped her. He gave Casey the impression that he'd wandered in off the street and hadn't a clue where he was.

Her impression turned out to be correct. Marcus Marriot, as he introduced himself, had come straight from the air-port to Cambridge. He'd been in Frankfurt, at the Book Fair, when he'd heard about Susannah, but now that he was here he wasn't quite sure of what to do next.

'Are you anybody?' he said.

It was a bit early for metaphysical debates, Casey thought.

'I mean, can you help me in any way? I'm Susannah's agent — and friend, too — you see.'

It occurred to her that Susannah Storey's death had been in the hands of the media for nearly twenty-four hours and this was the first person who'd turned up and claimed to be a friend. Though, in her experience, friends didn't usually take fifteen per cent of your earnings and expect your gratitude.

After introducing herself, Casey quickly told him everything she considered he needed to know. The scent of his powerful cologne, mingled with the smell of bacon from the dining room, was proving to be overpowering, and she was overcome with a strong desire to run outside and fill her lungs with some fresh air. Then John

McGrath, stinking of cigarette smoke, strode through the main doors.

'We got him, Casey!'

McGrath came towards her, completely ignoring Marcus Marriot, who, for all he knew, could have been a tabloid reporter.

Quickly, Casey introduced the two men. McGrath gave Marriot the dirty look he bestowed on anyone who enunciated the English language in a way that suggested a privileged education, but Marriot was much too agitated to notice.

'I heard they found her manuscript in the water with her, and I need to know if that's true.'

Taking out a red handkerchief from his breast pocket, he mopped his brow with a flamboyant gesture. 'She only ever keeps — kept — one copy, you see. Hand-written. Hates — hated — computers.'

So that was the way the land lay, Casey mused. He wasn't grieving for Susannah; he just wanted to know if he was going to get his cut. This was his high-earning client's very last novel, and he stood to make an even bigger fortune from her now that she was dead. But not if it was illegible and there wasn't a back-up anywhere.

Ignoring Marriot, Casey turned to McGrath. 'You've got Josh Hathaway?' she said.

'But not for murder. His alibi stands up.'

Although there was the small matter of drug dealing, a gleeful McGrath informed her. They had CCTV footage of him exchanging wraps for money on several different occasions during the time he was at Groove. His men were on their way to pick him up.

★ ★ ★

Was it possible to change your mind so many times about one person in such a short time? Danuta had started off believing she was falling in love with Josh. In a foreign land, he'd been the first person to make her laugh. Then, she'd hated him. He was arrogant, disrespectful of his mother, a liar and thief. He was still all those things — she hadn't changed her mind about that. But when he'd come knocking on her door last night, straight from the police station, she'd seen another side to him. He was frightened and he didn't know what to do.

The police were on to him, he told her. That McGrath was determined to get him for something, and if he couldn't lock him up for murder, he'd bust him for dealing, for sure, since there must be tape after tape of him selling wraps at Groove — and McGrath had promised to have every single one of those tapes thoroughly checked.

Danuta had made him coffee and tried to calm him down as best she could. She could never love him now, she decided, only pity him. Maybe it was because she realised that Josh no longer had the power to break her heart that she took him into her bed.

When she woke next morning, it was to see Josh, propping himself up on one arm and staring down at her.

'How long have you been doing that?' she asked sleepily.

'Ages,' he said. 'I've been thinking. I've got something — for when McGrath arrests me.'

Puzzled, she furrowed her brow.

'You know, I give them some information and they chop my sentence in half. On Saturday, when you saw me take Naomi's bag — '

'You were returning it, right?'

'Wrong. I was after her purse. Although it was a big wallet, actually. I went through all these different compartments, looking for notes.'

Danuta gave a disappointed sigh.

'But I found something else.'

'What?'

'Something that might tell them who killed Susannah Storey,' he replied.

3

Lady Violet Hathaway knelt before the fire in the living room of The Lodge and gazed, enchanted, at the flames. Lucky in a way that she'd caught that TV interview the other night, she thought. How indiscreet of Susannah to confide her writing methods to the interviewer — and several million viewers besides!

One copy and one copy only. Handwritten. So precious it travelled everywhere with her. The contents kept secret even from her agent until she'd placed the final full stop.

On Saturday, after Susannah had given her little speech declaring the new pool open, and cut the ribbon, Lady Violet had been unable to restrain herself. She had to know if her suspicions about the contents of this latest novel were correct. With a title like *Town And Gown*, and with Susannah's own admission on air that it dealt with a scandal from her own time at Cambridge, what else was Violet meant to think?

She'd spotted a gap between the sycophants who were queuing up to tell Susannah how wonderful she was and finally managed to corner her former student.

Brushing aside the usual courtesies, she'd said, 'I saw you being interviewed on TV last night.'

'Lady Vi!'

She'd hoped to intimidate Susannah by cutting straight to the chase, but Susannah had sharpened up since her student days. Violet blanched at the name. No one ever called her Vi. Not even Josh. Before she could stop her, Susannah had managed a peck on each cheek. When Violet tried to pull away, Susannah held on to her.

'If you think you're going to wangle the plot of *Town And Gown* out of me before I've shown it to my agent . . . ' she murmured in Violet's ear.

'I think I can guess the plot already,' Violet hissed back. 'Just remember, I have an extremely good lawyer.'

Susannah released her then and stepped back with a nonchalant toss of her glossy head.

'And I have a team of them who go through my manuscripts with a fine-toothed comb.' The chill in her reply was worthy of Lady Violet herself. 'Just remember, it's fiction I write. Fiction that sells by the cartload, by the way — not dry, academic tomes that no one ever reads.' Susannah's smile dripped poison. 'And in fiction it's not unusual for a character to cut short an innocent man's life in a car accident, because he thinks he's above the law,' she added. 'If you want to infer it's your poor dear dead husband I'm writing about, that's entirely up to you.'

'Stephen didn't think he was above the law,' Violet snapped.

Aware that her voice was rising, she checked the volume. Someone was looking her way — the pregnant detective that Eleanor had invited. She immediately turned her back to block her.

'Oh, really? I could have sworn the inquest revealed that Stephen had been ordered by his GP not to drive, because he had a degenerative disease,' Susannah countered. 'And that his licence had been taken away from him, because he'd already had a couple of brushes with the traffic police.'

Violet couldn't argue, because the fact was, Susannah was right. Stephen shouldn't have gone out in the car that day. She should have hidden the keys. God knows, she'd threatened to often enough.

But the truth was that she craved time to herself — rare, since Stephen's illness had been diagnosed. It had been a relief to be free of him some days, even if only for an hour while Josh napped and she could get on with her 'precious research,' as Stephen called it.

'When he drove into that pedestrian, it was because his foot slipped off the brake. The judge gave him a lenient sentence, remember,' she said.

'Only because he was already under sentence of death,' Susannah countered. 'Didn't he die six months afterwards? Pity that a healthy man in his prime had to lose his life, too, though.'

'I paid for that,' Violet said, furious now. 'With my promotion. That car accident was nothing to do with me and yet that's how the University Board decided that perhaps I wasn't quite the right figurehead for a ladies' college.'

'You got it in the end, though, didn't you?'

'And I want to keep it,' Violet snapped.

She'd worked and lobbied hard over ten long years to reach the position of Dean. How long would it be before people put two and two together about exactly who it was that Susannah Storey was describing in her novel? Then it would all begin again. The snide comments and sidelong looks, and the soft whispers that a person is always guilty by association quickly turning into a clamour that would eventually drum her out.

'This time I have my son to think about,' she added. 'He knows nothing about his father's accident.'

'And what else does he know nothing about?'

Light glanced off the blue water, the backdrop framing Susannah's elegant figure. Violet had never been so angry. Susannah had freely admitted she couldn't swim, even as she'd hacked through the ribbon with the pair of blunt scissors Naomi had handed over earlier. It was all Violet could do not to push her backwards straight into the pool. Except there'd be too many volunteers to jump in after her and fish her out.

'You've put it all in this book of yours then, have you?' Her voice had begun to tremble. 'Not just the accident but Stephen's affairs and his drunkenness?'

'Oh, Vi! I can't possibly tell you that,' Susannah smirked. 'You'll just have to buy the book like everyone else, when it comes out!'

With that, she turned her eyes away from Violet as yet another fan hoved into view.

Tossing one more crumpled page on to the fire, Violet thought about the manner of Susannah's death. Drowning was one of the very worst ways to go. Hit over the head with a bottle first, they said, with pages and pages of her novel floating on the water.

She wasn't going to argue with them. That pregnant detective wasn't as bovine as she looked, dropping by on the pretext of a social call last night, then, just as it looked as if she was on the point of leaving, casually asking why she'd been arguing with Susannah at the reception.

She certainly didn't want *her* round again. It wasn't beyond the realms of possibility she might discover that Violet, still furious, had gone straight from the pool and let herself into Susannah's room with the master key, knowing full well the famous author would be far too tied up with fans to leave the party for hours yet. It had only been the work of moments to locate the manuscript and walk the short distance back to The Lodge with it slipped inside her bag.

What those other sheets of paper found floating in the pool had been she had no idea and, frankly, she couldn't have cared less. She smiled now as she watched the charred words crumble in the flames and Susannah Storey's manuscript disappear for ever.

Naomi chewed the tip of her pen. Her bags were already lined up by the door ready for her departure. She couldn't stay now, after what had happened. Not someone with *her* fragile nerves. They couldn't possibly make her.

Naomi's fiancé had died tragically. She had been tipped over the edge and this was her first job since her recovery — offered to her by Lady Violet, who felt sorry for her.

What would Toby write, she wondered, as she re-read the letter she'd just written? Not this clunky effort, for sure. Words had dripped from his fingers like honey from a spoon. The times she'd walked into a room and he'd ignored her, not through bad manners — Toby had been a gentleman through and through, a New Man even before New Men existed — but because he was so wrapped up in the novel that he was writing.

'You'd save your manuscript before you'd save me if ever a fire broke out in the flat,' had been her little joke.

That book had been his baby. Precious. Fragile. He'd poured his hopes and dreams into it. On his twenty-fifth birthday, which coincided with the day he'd written *the end* on the final page, she'd given him his present.

He'd peered at the cheque made out for two hundred pounds to an editorial guidance service.

'Think of it as a stepping stone on the journey to getting your novel published,' she'd said.

For a fee, she'd explained, the agency offered a full critique of would-be authors' manuscripts. Act on their advice and suggestions and the manuscript would soon be polished enough to send to an agent. And how many times had Toby complained that the only way to get your novel published was through an intermediary?

'They're all published writers at this place,' she added, showing him the advert in the literary supplement of the Sunday paper that had caught her eye. 'Or at the very least, they're all writers on the cusp of a brilliant career themselves.'

Toby hadn't earned any money in a long time. He'd given up his job to finish this book. He'd never have been able to afford to take this step without her.

'You'd do this for me?' His eyes had shone with happiness.

'I've even addressed the label and bought this huge envelope to put it in,' she'd said, laying it down in front of him.

That had been the last time she'd ever seen Toby truly happy.

★ ★ ★

Casey had been summoned to the Fellows' Library. The WPC who came to collect her said that Josh Hathaway would speak only to 'that pregnant policeman'. They both smiled. He'd been charged with dealing Class A drugs, but he wanted to plea bargain, the officer said.

She barely had time to cross the threshold before Josh Hathaway was out of his chair, thrusting a purse and some papers into Casey's hand. DI John McGrath, perched on the edge of his seat, flexed his booted feet, calves trembling, like a greyhound at the trap. 'Encroaching on my patch again,' his look seemed to say.

'OK, I stole the purse but when you see what it contains, you'll realise what a big favour I've done you all,' Josh said. 'The letter's from her fiancé's mother. It was in the purse, alongside this photo and the newspaper article.'

McGrath craned his neck to see better. The purse was of soft black leather, with piping round the edges and a number of different compartments.

Casey glanced at the dog-eared photo. It was a head and shoulders shot of a young man, his expression distant, as if his mind was on higher things. Something about his hairstyle dated him.

Next, she carefully unfolded the sheet of newsprint.

'Did you tear this?'

'I didn't mean to,' he said. 'But it's old. You can see the date . . . '

Casey was already halfway through the piece. She raised her hand for silence. This was important. It took all her concentration. She read it quickly before moving on to the letter, then she read them both again, more carefully this time.

Her blood began to pound in her ears. She couldn't make sense of either piece of writing. But there was someone at Doughty Hall who could. Without a backward glance, she fled from the room. She barely heard McGrath's gruff, 'You can't just take off like that. This is my case, not yours,' or Josh Hathaway's plaintive, 'But how does this affect my sentence?'

* * *

When Casey burst into Naomi's room, she was scrabbling inside her handbag. She looked worried.

'Looking for this, Naomi?'

Casey held up the purse. Naomi's face relaxed, then tightened again. She'd realised the implications, Casey guessed.

'Money's all here, you'll be glad to know,' Casey went on. 'And there's a couple of other things you might be missing, too.'

'Give me that!'

If Casey had hitherto failed to think about her safety, given her advanced state of pregnancy, she did so now.

'Let me read something to you first.' Her buoyant tone belied her fear. What if Naomi reached for something to attack her with? Casey had never been so pleased to see McGrath bursting in through the door, the WPC close behind.

'Just in time to hear the coroner' report on Toby Reid, dated the eighteenth of July 1988.'

She flashed the dog-eared photograph at Naomi, relief flooding through her. 'He was your fiancé, wasn't he, Naomi?'

Naomi said nothing, simply glared. McGrath and the WPC had been joined by Josh Hathaway, Danuta, and Eleanor Humphreys, who brought up the rear.

Casey began to read out loud.

'A verdict of suicide, while of unsound mind, was brought today in the case of Toby Reid, aged twenty-five, of Cambridge. According to his fiancé, Naomi Dodd, Mr Reid, unemployed, had fallen into a deep depression after the novel that had taken five years of his life to write had

been mercilessly slated by a reader at an editorial guidance service.

'Toby had given up his job to write,' Miss Dodd, aged twenty-two, told the coroner. 'I encouraged him to get professional advice before submitting it for publication and actually paid quite a large amount of money, though I didn't begrudge him this at all — it was his birthday present from me. We were both excited when the report came back, but if I was devastated to read the harsh words it contained, then Toby was plunged into the depths of despair.'

'Miss Dodd broke down at the inquest and was escorted back to the private psychiatric hospital where she has been undergoing therapy for a condition brought on by her fiancé's suicide. 'I blame myself,' she said, as she was led, sobbing, from the courtroom.'

McGrath stepped forward and Casey handed him the news report.

'Interesting,' he said.

'It gets better,' Casey said. 'This letter is from Toby's mother. Dated a couple of months ago, when she heard that Naomi had been successful in her interview for the position of bursar, here at Doughty Hall. Care to read it? I must admit, my back's giving me a bit of gyp. Wouldn't mind a sit-down.'

While Casey sank down into the nearest chair, Naomi remained upright and expressionless. In a monotone, McGrath read Mrs Reid's brief and carefully worded letter out loud.

It began with congratulations that Naomi had finally been successful in getting a job after so many disappointments. Mrs Reid knew Doughty Hall and imagined Naomi would feel safe in such an environment. There was news of her own life and one or two snippets about the garden and the cat who'd recently had kittens.

The letter ended thus: *I'm so glad you've decided to let bygones be bygones at long last. The grudge you bore that dreadful, insensitive, callous woman, who wrote the reader's report on poor Toby's novel, has been standing between you and full recovery for so many years now. But in your last letter, it was as if you'd suddenly decided to move on with your life. With all my heart, dear Naomi, I truly believe that this is what darling Toby would have wanted for you.*

'Dreadful, insensitive and callous woman,' he quoted from memory, having carefully replaced the letter inside the envelope. 'Now, who could that be, I wonder?'

'If you don't mind, I've papers to urgently see to,' Naomi glanced nervously towards her desk.

It was a futile gesture to lunge for the scissors. Even if she'd managed to reach them before the WPC and McGrath between them succeeded in intercepting her, they wouldn't have inflicted much damage. Casey recognised them as the blunt pair that Susannah had taken such a long time to saw through the ribbon with on Saturday.

★ ★ ★

Naomi Dodd made her confession in the Fellows' Library. Getting the job at Doughty Hall had been part of the scheme she'd long plotted to get her own back on Susannah Storey, she said.

'It was *her* name that appeared at the bottom of the foul report she returned to Toby,' she said. 'She must have been working there while she waited to hear that her first novel had found a publisher. As soon as I got this job I lobbied for her to be the celebrity to open the pool. I knew she'd come. The letter I sent her agent was so fawning, she wouldn't have been able to resist.'

'Did you plan to kill her, Naomi?' asked Casey.

'I wasn't sure at first,' she said. 'I think I just wanted to remind her of Toby, and what she'd done to make him take his life. I think, at first, I just wanted to remind her of Toby's manuscript and her report.'

'So what tipped you over?' McGrath wanted to know.

'Simple. She said she had no memory, either of reading the book or writing the report. One awful book was much the same as another, she said, and she should know because she'd read a few.'

Casey had only been briefly introduced to Susannah on Saturday. 'Flashy', was how she'd thought of her then. When the witness at the bus stop had described how she'd taken on Josh Hathaway, she'd added 'bossy'. But after hearing this from Naomi, 'cruel', 'insensitive' and 'heartless' joined the list of adjectives.

Even so, had these words merited being hit on the head with a bottle of wine; then, when she'd lost her footing and slid into the water, left to struggle till she drowned? She didn't think so and she said so, too.

'I might have walked away, you know,' Naomi said, after considering Casey's words. 'But, when I quoted one line of her report, she laughed. As if it were the wittiest line anyone had ever written. I'm afraid I had to let her have it then.'

★ ★ ★

'Tell me again,' said Dom. 'What exactly did this — what was her name? — give as her excuse for chucking a bottle at Susannah Storey, pushing her in the water and leaving her to drown?'

Casey was home at last. Feet up, cup of

tea in hand, provided by her partner, who was gratifyingly pleased to see her back home. The prospect of a hot bath and an early night beckoned seductively. There was one fly in the ointment, however. But she hadn't quite decided how to deal with that one yet.

'Naomi Dodd,' she said. 'She quoted a line from Susannah Storey's report. *Why on earth would you imagine that anyone in their right mind, with any sort of reputation in literary circles, would want to publish this dreadful book?*'

Dom shook his head in disbelief. Casey stared at the walls. And then at the ceiling. She was surrounded by beige. She thought she had expressly told Dom that she really didn't care what he did with the house while she was away, as long as he didn't paint it beige. Or had she just thought it?

'So, what do you think of my decorating skills?'

Was it Oscar Wilde, on his deathbed, who'd said of his room's wallpaper, 'One or other of us has to go'? But she was too tired to fight and so she said it was fine.

'You hate it, don't you?'

Dom looked her straight in the eye. There was no way now she could wriggle out of this one.

'Not hate,' she hedged. 'Hate's far too strong a word. But . . . Well, don't you think it's just a little bit too *beige*?'

Dom looked startled. 'Beige? It's never beige! It's ivory. I thought you'd like it. It's tasteful and you can put lots of different colours with it.'

He was hurt. Mortified by her remark, obviously. How easily a careless word could wound. But you'd have to be as damaged as Naomi Dodd to let it stay with you for almost twenty years. Still, she didn't want to risk Dom plotting to do her in, just because she hated his colour scheme. Then she had a brainwave.

'I love it, personally. Honest, Dom. But, well, I'm just thinking about the baby becoming a toddler and all the dirty fingerprints it's bound to leave all over everywhere.'

Dom considered her words. She'd convinced him. She could see it in his eyes.

'You know,' he said. He took her feet in his hands and began to rub them gently in the way he knew she loved. 'I hadn't thought about that. You're right. It's totally the wrong colour for a child-friendly home.'

'So we'll change it, then?'

'Yes,' he said, letting her feet go. 'Lucky I miscalculated, though. There's enough left for the kitchen and the bathroom, too. There may even be some over to paint your office.'

He made another grab for her feet and set about tickling them remorselessly till she squealed for him to stop.

'Only if you tell the truth, Casey Clunes,' he yelled.

'OK, OK, I hate it!' she squealed.

She could never love a man she could hoodwink, she thought, as, finally, Dom stopped tickling her feet and began to concentrate on kissing her instead.

THE END

We do hope that you have enjoyed reading this large print book.

Did you know that all of our titles are available for purchase?

We publish a wide range of high quality large print books including:
Romances, Mysteries, Classics
General Fiction
Non Fiction and Westerns

Special interest titles available in large print are:
The Little Oxford Dictionary
Music Book, Song Book
Hymn Book, Service Book

Also available from us courtesy of Oxford University Press:
Young Readers' Dictionary
(large print edition)
Young Readers' Thesaurus
(large print edition)

For further information or a free brochure, please contact us at:
Ulverscroft Large Print Books Ltd.,
The Green, Bradgate Road, Anstey,
Leicester, LE7 7FU, England.
Tel: (00 44) **0116 236 4325**
Fax: (00 44) **0116 234 0205**